Every Time We Say Goodbye

Kristina McMorris

W F HOWES LTD

This large print edition published in 2012 by
W F Howes Ltd
Unit 4, Rearsby Business Park, Gaddesby Lane,
Rearsby, Leicester LE7 4YH

1 3 5 7 9 10 8 6 4 2

First published in the United Kingdom in 2012
by HarperCollins Publishers

A CIP catalogue record for this book is available
from the British Library

ISBN 978 1 47120 435 7

Typeset by Palimpsest Book Production Limited,
Falkirk, Stirlingshire
Printed and bound in Great Britain
by MPG Books Ltd, Bodmin, Cornwall

MIX
Paper from
responsible sources
FSC
www.fsc.org
FSC® C018575

*For those whose voices stayed silent
so that one day others could sing*

PART I

Every leaf while on its tree sways in unison;
bears the same light and shadow,
is sustained by the same sap that will release
  it in blazing color.

It is that moment before falling we all live for,
to see ourselves for the first time,
to hear our name being called from the inside.

—Deanna Nikaido,
daughter of a Japanese American 'evacuee'

CHAPTER 1

November 1941
Los Angeles, California

At the sound of her brother's voice, flutters of joy turned to panic in Maddie Kern. 'Cripes,' she whispered, perched on her vanity seat. 'What's he doing home?'

Jo Allister, her closest girlfriend and trusted lookout, cracked open the bedroom door. She peeked into the hall as TJ hollered again from downstairs.

'Maddie! You here?'

It was six o'clock on a Friday. He should have been at his campus job all night. If he knew who was about to pick her up for a date . . .

She didn't want to imagine what he would do.

Maddie scanned the room, seeking a solution amidst her tidy collection of belongings – framed family photos on the bureau, her posters of the New York Symphony, of Verdi's *Aida* at the Philharmonic. But even her violin case, which she'd defended from years of dings and scratches, seemed to shake its head from the corner and say,

3

Six months of sneaking around and you're surprised this would happen?

Jo closed the door without a click and pressed her back against the knob. 'Want me to keep him out?' Her pale lips angled with mischief. Despite the full look of her figure, thanks to her baggy hardware store uniform, she was no match for TJ's strength. Only his stubbornness.

'My brother seeing *me* isn't the problem,' Maddie reminded her. She glanced at the clock on her nightstand, and found cause for remaining calm. 'Lane shouldn't be here for another twelve minutes. If I can just—'

The faint sound of an engine drove through the thought and parked on her words. Had he shown up early? She raced to the window, where she swatted away her childhood drapes. She threw the pane upward and craned her neck. Around the abandoned remains of her father's Ford, she made out a wedge of the street. No sign of Lane's car. She still had time.

'Hey, Rapunzel,' Jo said. 'You haven't turned batty enough to scale walls for a fella, have you?'

Maddie shushed her, interrupted by creaks of footfalls on the staircase. '*You* have to do it,' she decided.

'Do what?'

Warn Lane, Maddie was about to say, but realized she needed to talk to him herself, in order to set plans to meet later that night. Come tomorrow, he'd be on a train back to Stanford.

She amended her reply. 'You've got to distract TJ for me.'

Jo let out a sharp laugh. Pushing out her chest, she tossed back stragglers from her ash-brown ponytail. 'What, with all my stylish locks and hefty bosom?' Then she muttered, 'Although, based on his past girlfriends, I suppose that's all it would take.'

'No, I mean – you both love baseball. Chat about that.'

Jo raised a brow at her.

'Please,' Maddie begged. 'You came by to help me get ready, didn't you? So, *help* me.'

'Why not just tell him and get it over with?'

'Because you know how he feels about my dating.' *A distraction from her future,* he called it. The same theory he applied to his own career.

'Maddie. This isn't just about any guy.'

'I know, I know, and I'll come clean. But not yet.'

A knuckle-rap sounded on her door. 'You in there?'

She sang out, 'Hold on a minute,' and met Jo's eyes. '*Please.*'

Jo hesitated before releasing a sigh that said Maddie would owe her one. A big one.

'I'll come right back,' Maddie promised, 'once I head Lane off down the block.'

After a grumble, Jo pasted on a smile, wide enough for a dentist's exam, and flung open the door. 'TJ,' she exclaimed, 'how 'bout that streak of DiMaggio's, huh?'

Behind his umber bangs, his forehead creased in puzzlement. 'Uh, yeah. That was . . . somethin'.' His hand hung from a loop of his cuffed jeans. Nearly four years of wash and wear had frayed the patch on his *USC Baseball* sweatshirt. Its vibrancy had long ago faded, just like TJ's.

Diverting from Jo's unsubtle approach, Maddie asked him, 'Didn't you have to work tonight?'

'I was supposed to, but Jimmy needed to switch shifts this weekend.' His cobalt gaze suddenly narrowed and gripped hers. 'You going somewhere special?'

'What?' She softly cleared her throat before thinking to glance down at her flared navy dress, her matching strappy heels. She recalled the pin curls in her auburn, shoulder-length do. The ensemble didn't spell out a casual trip to a picture show.

Jo swiftly interjected, 'There's a new hot jazz band playing at the Dunbar. They say Duke Ellington and Billie Holiday might even be there. I'm dragging Maddie along. A keen study in music. You know, for her big audition.'

'I thought you were practicing tonight,' he said to Maddie.

'I am – I will. After we get back.'

'You two going alone?'

'We'll be fine.' As everything would be, if he'd let up long enough.

'All right,' he said, rubbing the back of his neck. 'I'll just grab a bite in the kitchen then come along.'

Maddie stifled a gasp. 'No, really. You don't have to.'

'At the Dunbar? Oh yeah I do.'

Criminy. Was he going to hold her hand as they crossed the street to reach the bus stop too?

'TJ, this is ridiculous. I'm nineteen years old. Dad used to let us go out all the—'

He lashed back with a fistful of words. 'Well, Dad's gone, and I'm not him. You don't like the deal, you can stay home.'

Stunned, Maddie stared at him. He'd spoken the word *gone* as though their father had died along with their mother.

Jo waved her hands, shooing away the tension. 'So it's settled. We'll all go together.' Maddie widened her eyes as Jo continued, 'And hey, while he's eating, you'll have time to drop off your neighbor's letter. The one the postman delivered by accident.'

The letter . . .?

Confusion quickly gave way to disappointment. Maddie now had an excuse to sneak out, but only to cancel rather than delay her date with Lane. She hated the prospect of missing one of his rare visits from school.

On the upside, in two weeks he would be back for winter break, offering more opportunities for quality time together.

'Fine, then,' she snipped at her brother. 'Come if you want.'

What other choice did she have?

While Jo bombarded TJ with questions about the World Series, Maddie strode down the hall. Her urge to sprint mounted as she recalled the time. She made it as far as the bottom step when the doorbell rang.

Oh, God.

'I'll get it!' She rushed to the entry. Hoping to prevent the disaster from worsening, she opened the door only halfway. Yet at the greeting of Lane's perfect white smile, all her worries evaporated like mist. The warm glow of the portico light caressed his short black hair and olive skin. Shadows swooped softly from his high cheekbones. His almond-shaped eyes, inherited from his Japanese ancestors, shone with the same deep brown that had reached out and captured her heart the first time he'd held her last spring, an innocent embrace that had spiraled into more.

'Hi, Maddie,' he said, and handed her a bouquet of lavender lilies. Their aroma was divine, nearly hypnotic, just like his voice.

But then footsteps on the stairs behind her sobered her senses.

'You have to go,' was all she got out before TJ called to him.

'Tomo!' It was the nickname he'd given Lane Moritomo when they were kids. 'You didn't tell me you were coming home.'

The startle in Lane's eyes deftly vanished as his best friend approached.

Maddie edged herself aside. Her heart thudded

in the drum of her chest as she watched Lane greet him with a swift hug. A genuine grin lit TJ's face, a rare glimpse of the brother she missed.

'I'm only in till tomorrow,' Lane told him. 'Then it's straight back for classes.' Though several inches shorter than TJ, he emitted a power in his presence, highlighted by his tailored black suit.

'Term's almost over,' TJ remarked. 'What brought you back?'

'There was a funeral this afternoon. Had to go with my family.'

Surprisingly, TJ's expression didn't tense at the grim topic. Then again, Lane always did have the ability – even after the accident – to settle him when no one else could. 'Anyone I know?'

'No, no. Just the old geezer who ran the bank before my dad. Came away with some nice flowers at least.' Lane gestured to the lilies Maddie had forgotten were in her grip. 'Priest said they didn't have space for them all.'

TJ brushed over the gift with a mere glance. 'I was gonna take the girls to some jazz joint. Any chance you wanna come?'

'Sure. I'd love to,' he said, not catching the objection in Maddie's face.

Her gaze darted to the top of the staircase, seeking help. There, she found Jo leaning against the rail with a look that said, *Ah, well, things could be worse.*

And she was right. Before the night was over, things could get much, much worse.

CHAPTER 2

Cigarette smoke at the Dunbar swirled, adding to the fog of Lane's thoughts. Since arriving, he had been struggling to keep his focus on the Negroes playing riffs onstage. Now, with TJ off fetching drinks, he could finally allow his eyes to settle on the profile of Maddie, seated across from him. Her jasmine perfume, while subtle, somehow transcended the wafts of beer and sweat in the teeming club.

From above the bar, blue lights danced over the crowd united in music and laughter – racially integrated, as the entire world would be when Lane was done with it – and rippled shadows across Maddie's face. The narrow slope of her nose led to full lips, moist with a red sheen. Her hazel eyes studied the musicians with such intensity that he chose to merely watch her.

Amazing that he'd known her for more than half his life, yet only months ago had he truly begun to see her. The ache to touch her swelled, along with a desire to make up for lost time. He reached over and brushed the back of her creamy hand resting on their cocktail table.

She jolted, her trance broken. 'Sorry,' she said, and returned his smile.

'Pretty good, isn't he?' Lane indicated the saxophonist. The long, haunting notes of 'Summertime' made the guy's talent obvious even to Lane.

'Yeah, I suppose.'

'You don't think so?'

'No, I do. It's just – the structure's so loose, with all those slurs, and the downbeat going in and out. Plus, the key changes are too quick to feel grounded. And during the chorus, his timing keeps—' She broke off, her nose crinkling in embarrassment. 'Gosh, listen to me. I sound like a royal snob, don't I?'

'Not at all.'

She exaggerated a squint. 'Liar.'

They both laughed. In truth, he could listen to her talk forever. 'God, I've missed you,' he said to her.

'I've missed you too.' The sincerity in her voice was so deep, he could lose himself in that sound for days. But a moment later, she glanced around as if abruptly aware of the surrounding spectators, and her glimmering eyes dulled, turned solid as her defenses. She slid her hand away, sending a pang down his side.

He told himself not to read into it, that her aversion to a public show of affection wasn't a matter of race. She was simply fearful of jeopardizing her relationship with her brother. Understandable, after all she had been through.

11

'So,' she said. 'Where did Jo go?'

'To the ladies' room.'

'Oh.'

Awkwardness stretched between them as the song came to a close. They joined in with a round of applause. When the next ballad began, it occurred to him that a slow dance would be their only chance for a private, uninterrupted talk. His only chance to hold her tonight. He gestured to the dance floor. 'Shall we?'

'I . . . don't think we should.'

'Maddie, your brother won't get any ideas just because—'

A booming voice cut him off. 'Evenin', sweet cakes.' The guy sidled up to the table near Maddie, a familiar look to him. Beer sloshed in his mug, only two fingers gripping the handle. He had the sway of someone who'd already downed a few. 'Fancy seeing you here.'

Maddie shifted in her seat, her look of unease growing. 'Hi, Paul.'

Now Lane remembered him. Paul Lamont. The guy was a baseball teammate of TJ's, ever since their high school years, subjecting Lane to occasional encounters as a result. Even back then, the tow-head had carried a torch for Maddie subtle as a raging bonfire.

'What do you say?' Paul licked his bottom lip and leaned on the table toward her. 'Wanna cut a rug?'

'No thanks.'

'C'mon, doll. You don't wanna hurt my feelings, do ya?'

Lane couldn't hold back. 'I think the lady's answered.'

Paul snapped his gaze toward the challenge. He started to reply when recognition caught. 'Well, lookee here. Lane Moratoro.' Beer dove from his mug, splashed on Lane's dress shoes.

'It's Moritomo.' Lane strove to be civil, despite being certain the error was purposeful.

'Oh, that's right. Mo-ree-to-mo.' Then Paul yelled, 'Hey, McGhee!'

A guy standing nearby twisted around. His fitted orange shirt and broad nose enhanced his lumberjack's build. 'Yeah, what?'

'Got another rich Oriental here who wants to rule our country. Thinks he's gonna be the first Jap governor of – no, wait.' Paul turned to Lane. 'It's a *senator*, right?'

Lane clenched his hands under the table. 'Something like that.' Out of the corner of his eye, he glimpsed Maddie shaking her head in a stiff, just-ignore-him motion.

Paul's lips curled into a wry grin. 'Well, in that case, maybe you can help a local citizen out.' He put an unwelcome hand on Lane's shoulder. 'See, my pop's been truck farming for twenty-some years, working his fingers to the bone. But wouldn't you know it? Jap farmers round here just keep undercutting his damn prices. So I was thinkin', when you're elected senator you could do

13

something about that.' His mouth went taut. 'Or would your *real* loyalty be with those dirty slant eyes?'

Lane shot to his feet, tipping his chair onto the floor. He took a step forward, but a grasp pulled at his forearm.

'Lane.' It was Maddie at his side. 'Let it go.' The lumberjack squared his shoulders as she implored, 'Honey, forget him. He's not worth it.'

At that, Paul's glance ricocheted between her and Lane. He scoffed in disbelief. 'Don't tell me you two are . . .'

Lane knew he should deny it for Maddie's sake, yet the words failed to form. Again, her touch slipped away, leaving the skin under his sleeve vacantly cold.

Paul snorted a laugh, thick with disgust. 'Well, Christ Almighty. Who'd a thought.'

Lane's nails bit into his palms. He felt his upper back muscles gather, cinching toward the cords of his neck.

'We got a problem here?' TJ arrived at the scene and put down their drinks.

'Everything's great,' Maddie announced. 'Isn't it, fellas.'

Jitterbug notes failed to cushion their silence.

'Paul?' TJ said.

Paul nodded tightly and replied, 'Just fine, Kern. I'm surprised, is all. Figured you'd be more selective about who made moves on your little sister.'

TJ's face turned to stone. 'What are you sayin'?'

Once more, a denial refused to budge from Lane's throat.

'What, you didn't know either?' Paul said, but TJ didn't respond. With a glint of amusement, Paul shook his head, right as Jo returned to their table. 'Goes to prove my point,' he went on. 'Every one of them filthy yellow Japs is a double-crosser, no matter how well you think you—'

His conclusion never reached the air. A blow from TJ's fist stuffed it back into the bastard's mouth. Paul's beer mug dropped to the floor, arcing a spray across strangers' legs. Shrieks outpoured in layers.

A wall of orange moved closer; McGhee the lumberjack wanted in on the action. Lane lurched forward to intervene. Diplomacy deferred, he shoved the guy with an adrenaline charge that should have at least rocked the guy backward, but McGhee was a mountain. Solid, unmovable. A mountain with a punch like Joe Louis. His hit launched a searing explosion into Lane's eye socket.

The room spun, a carousel ride at double speed. Through his good eye, Lane spied the ground. He was hunched over but still standing. He raised his head an inch and glimpsed TJ taking an uppercut to the jaw. TJ came right back with a series of pummels to Paul's gut.

Lane strained to function in the dizzy haze, to slow the ride. He noted McGhee's legs planted beside him. The thug motioned for Lane to rise

15

for a second round. Before going back in, though, Lane was bringing support. His fingers closed on the legs of a wooden chair. He swung upward, knocking McGhee over a table and into a stocky colored man, who then grabbed him by the orange collar.

'Cops!' someone hollered.

And the music stopped.

'Let's scram, Tomo!' In an instant, TJ was towing him by the elbow. They threaded through the chaos with Maddie and Jo on their heels. They didn't stop until reaching an empty alley several blocks away.

Lane bent over, hands on his thighs, to catch his breath. The echo of his pulse pounded in his ears, throbbed his swelling eye. Still, through it all he heard laughter. TJ's laughter. That carefree sound had been as much a part of Lane's childhood as Japanese Saturday school, or strawberry malts at Tilly's Diner.

Maddie rolled her eyes with a glower. 'Well, I'm glad *someone* thinks that was funny.'

'See, I was right.' Jo nudged her arm. 'Told you that joint was jumpin'.'

'Yeah,' she said, 'it was jumpin' all right. Too bad we almost jumped straight into a jail cell.' When TJ's laughter grew, Maddie's smile won out. She hit her brother lightly on the chest. 'You're off your nut.'

Lane grinned. 'And this is new news?'

Jo peeked out around the brick wall. Water

drizzled from a drain spout. 'Coast is clear,' she reported.

The ragged foursome treaded toward the bus stop. On the way, Lane turned to TJ and quietly offered his thanks – for what he did, for defending him.

'Eh,' TJ said, 'what're friends for.' He used a sleeve to wipe the trickle of blood from his lip, then slung an arm over Lane's shoulder. 'Besides, I can't think of the last time I had that much fun.'

The vision of TJ hammering out his aggressions on Paul came back in a flash of images. 'I'm just glad I'm not your enemy,' Lane said with a smile – one that faded the moment he recalled what had initially provoked the fight.

CHAPTER 3

It was on nights like this that Maddie missed her most, when her love life seemed a jumble of knots only a mother could untangle. More than that, her mom's advice would have fostered hopes of a happily ever after.

The woman had been nothing if not a romantic.

She'd adored roses and rainstorms and candlelight, in that order. She had declared chocolate an essential food for the heart, and poetry as replenishment for the soul. She'd kept every courtship note from her husband – who she'd sworn was more handsome than Clark Gable – and had no qualms about using her finest serving ware for non-holiday dinners. Life, she would say, was too short not to use the good china. As though she had known how short hers would be.

Maddie tugged her bathrobe over her cotton nightgown. Unfortunately, no amount of warmth would relax the wringing in her chest. Always this was the cost of remembering her mother. The one remedy Maddie could count on was music.

She placed the violin case on her bed. Unlatching the lid, she freed her instrument from its red

18

velvet–lined den. The smooth wood of the violin, of the bow, felt cool and wonderful in her hands. Like a crisp spring morning. Like air.

An audience of classical composers – black-and-white, wallet-sized portraits – sat poised in the lid's interior. Mozart, Mendelssohn, Bach, and Tchaikovsky peered with critical eyes. *Do our works justice, Miss Kern, or give us due cause to roll over in our graves.*

She rosined and tuned in systematic preparation. Then she positioned herself properly before the music stand. Bach's Partita No. 3 in E major. The sheets were aligned and ready. She knew them by heart but took no chances. She placed the chin rest at her jaw, inhaling the fragrance of the polished woodwork. A shiver of anticipation traveled through her.

Eyes intent on the prelude, she raised her bow over the bridge. Her internal metronome ticked two full measures of allegro tempo. Only then did she launch the horsehairs into action. Notes pervaded the room, precise and sharp. Her finger-tips rippled toward the scroll and down again, like a wave fighting its own current. The strings vibrated beneath her skin, the bow skipped under her control. And with each passing phrase, each conquered slur, the twisting on her heart loosened, the memories faded away.

By the time she reached the final note, the calculated stanzas had brought order back to her life. She held her pose in silence, waiting reluctantly for the world to reenter her consciousness.

'Maddie?'

Startled back, she turned toward the doorway.

'Just wanted to say good night.' Her brother held what appeared to be ice cubes bound by a dish-cloth on his right knuckles. His scuffle with Paul suddenly seemed days rather than hours ago. 'Got a game tomorrow morning. Then I'm taking Jimmy's shift,' he reminded her.

'Are you sure you can do all that, with your hand?'

He glanced down. 'Ah, it's nothin',' he said, lowering the injury to his side.

TJ's hand could be broken into a thousand pieces – as could his heart – and he'd never admit it.

'That sounded good, by the way,' he said. 'The song you were playing.'

She offered a smile. 'Thanks.'

'You using it for the audition?'

'I might. If I make it past the required pieces.'

'Well, don't sweat it. I know you're gonna get in next time.' In contrast to this past year, he meant, when she had blown the audition at I.M.A.

Under the Juilliard School of Music, the Institute of Musical Art had been established in New York to rival the best of European conserva-tories. Maddie's entrance into the program was a goal her dad had instilled in her since her ninth birthday. He'd gifted her with a used violin, marking the first time he had ever expressed grand hopes for *her* future, versus her brother's.

'You know, I was thinking. . . .' Maddie fidgeted with the end of her bow. 'When I visit Dad this week, you should come along.'

TJ's eyes darkened. 'I got a lot of stuff to do.'

'But, we could go any day you'd like.'

'I don't think so.'

'TJ,' she said wearily. 'He's been there a year and you haven't gone once. You can't avoid him forever.'

'*Wanna bet?*' Resentment toughened his voice, a cast shielding a wound – that wound being grief, Maddie was certain. She had yet to see him shed a tear over their mother's death, and those feelings had to have pooled somewhere.

After a long moment brimming with the unspoken, his expression softened. She told herself to hug him, a sign she understood. Yet the lie of that prevented her from moving. Their father, after all, had never even been charged. How many years would TJ continue to blame him?

TJ studied his ice bag and murmured, 'I'm just not ready, okay?'

Maddie knew better than to push him, mule-headed as he could be. Besides, she couldn't discount his admission, which held promise, if thin. And truth, the core of his existence.

'Fair enough.' She tried to smile, but the contrast of her ongoing deception soured her lips.

Lane.

Her steady.

It had been Maddie's idea to keep their courtship a secret, at least until the relationship developed. With TJ's temperament heightening along with his protectiveness of her, why get him hot and bothered for no reason? His friendship with Lane aside, society's resistance to mixed couples wouldn't have helped her case.

Tonight, though, from her brother's old smile to his old laugh, his defending Lane with gusto, she saw an opening for his approval. She needed to act before the opportunity closed.

'Well, good night,' TJ said, and angled away.

'Wait.'

He looked at her.

The words gathered in her throat, but none of them suitable for a brother. She didn't dare describe how a mere glance from Lane could make her feel more glamorous than a starlet. How his touch to her lower spine, while guiding her through a doorway, would cause a tingle beyond description.

'What is it?' TJ pressed.

Time to be square with him. She clutched her bow and hoped for the best. 'The thing that Paul said,' she began, 'about me and Lane . . . together . . .'

He shook his head. 'Ah, don't worry.'

'Yeah, but—'

'Maddie, it's fine.'

Stop interrupting, she wanted to yell. She had to get this out, to explain how one date had simply led to another. 'TJ, I need to tell you—'

'I already know.'

Her heart snagged on a beat. She reviewed his declaration, striving to hide her astonishment. 'You do?'

His mouth stretched into a wide grin. The sight opened pores of relief on her neck before she could question how he'd found out.

Of course . . . Lane must have told him. In which case, how long had her brother gone without saying so? All these months spent fretting for nothing. She couldn't decide which of them she wanted to smack, or embrace, more.

'Seriously,' TJ mused, 'the two of you dating? That's the stupidest thing I ever heard.' He bit off a laugh, and Maddie froze. 'Lane's part of our family – the only family we've got left. Even if he ever did get a wild hair to ask you out, he'd come to me first. He's not the kind to go behind a pal's back. Paul was just drunk, and he was egging for a fight. Don't let anything he said get to you, all right?'

The implication struck hard, shattering Maddie's confession. 'Right,' she breathed.

'Listen, I'd better hit the sack. Sleep well.'

'You too,' she said with a nod. Though with her uncertainties and emotions gearing up to battle, she expected anything but a restful sleep.

CHAPTER 4

'Shhh.' With a finger to his lips, Lane reminded his sister to keep as quiet as a ninja. Her analogy, not his. Emma gave him a conspiratorial smile. In her blouse and pleated skirt, black bob framing her round face, she stood next to him behind his bedroom door. Their secret quest lent a twinkle to her chocolate, Betty Boop eyes.

He donned his sunglasses, a necessary measure. Not as protection from the cloudy morning light, but to prevent a scolding should they fail to sneak past their mother. Although he felt rather proud of his inaugural fistfight, the bruises encircling his puffy left eye would hardly earn parental praise. At least Maddie wouldn't see him like this. His train would depart hours before she'd be off work.

Lane pushed aside his suitcase that barricaded the door. His clothes were packed, ready to nab once he and Emma returned, en route to the station. One cautious step at a time they crept down the hallway. The polished wood floor felt slick beneath his socks. Navigating a corner, hindered by his shaded view, he bumped something on the narrow table against the wall. Their mother's vase. The painted showpiece teetered. Its ghostly sparrow clung to a withered branch as Lane reached out, but Emma, lower to the ground, made the save.

He sighed and mouthed, *Thank you.*

Emma beamed.

They continued down the stairs. A Japanese folk song crackled on the gramophone in the formal room. The female singer warbled solemnly about cherry blossoms in spring and a longing to return to Osaka, the city of her birth.

It was no coincidence the tune was a favorite of Lane's mother.

From the closet in the *genkan*, their immaculate foyer, he retrieved his trench coat with minimal sound. His sister did the same with her rose-hued jacket. Their house smelled of broiled fish and bean-curd soup. The maid was preparing breakfast. Guilt eased into Lane over her wasted efforts, yet only a touch; he always did prefer pancakes and scrambled eggs.

He pulled out a brief note explaining their excursion, set it on the cabinet stocked with slippers for guests. Then he threw on his wingtips and handed Emma her saddle shoes. As she leaned over to put them on, coins rained from her pocket. This time she reached out too late. Pennies clattered on the slate floor.

'Get them later,' Lane urged in an undertone, and grabbed the door handle.

'*Doko ikun?*'

Lane bristled at his mother's inquiry. 'I'm . . . taking Emma to Santa Monica, to the Pleasure Pier. Remember, I mentioned it yesterday?' He risked a glance in his mother's direction to avert suspicion. Even in her casual plum housedress, Kumiko Moritomo was the epitome of elegance. Like an actress from a kabuki theatre, never was she seen without powder and lipstick applied, her ebony hair flawlessly coiffed. A small mole dotted her lower left cheek, as dainty as her frame, under-scoring the disparity of her chiseled expressions.

'*Asagohan tabenasai*,' she said to Emma.

'But, *Okāsan* . . .' The eight-year-old whined in earnest, an understandable reaction. What child would want to waste time eating breakfast? Cotton candy and carousel rides were at stake.

Their mother didn't bother with a verbal admon-ishment. Her steely glare was enough to send the girl cowering to the kitchen. '*Ohashi o chanto tsukainasai*,' their mother called out, Emma's daily reminder to use her chopsticks properly. Crossing the utensils, though it more easily picked up food, symbolized some nonsense involving death. One of many bad omens to avoid on the woman's tedious list of superstitions.

She shifted to Lane and jerked her chin toward the formal room. 'We have an issue to discuss,' she said in her native tongue. Despite having immigrated to America with her husband more than two decades ago, she spoke to them only in Japanese, which Lane now honored in return. The

26

show of obedience might help at least delay a stock lecture.

'Why don't we talk when Emma and I get back? Before the train. I did promise to take her this morning.'

'We will speak *now*.' She turned to fetch her husband from the den. Negotiating wasn't an option.

Why couldn't she have had a Mahjong game scheduled? Or her flower-arranging class? Either activity, required by her societal ranking, might have prevented whatever was to come.

Lane shucked off his shoes. In the formal room, he dropped into a wingback chair. The surrounding décor emanated a starkness that carried a chill. Decorative katana swords and encased figurines created a museum display of a heritage to which he felt little connection.

He bounced his heel on the ornate rug, checked his watch. Perhaps if he could guess the impending topic, he could speed things along. The laughing fit he and his sister had barely managed to contain at yesterday's funeral seemed the most likely possibility, given that the high hats of Little Tokyo had been in attendance.

But really, who could blame them?

Pretending to grieve for their father's predecessor, the widely despised manager of Sumitomo Bank, would have been hard enough without the suffocating incense and silly Buddhist rites. The frilly green dress their mother had forced Emma to wear – complete with an onslaught of matching gloves and bows – befit a Japanese Shirley Temple. The sole element lacking absurdity had been the priest's droning chant. Surely the audience would have fallen asleep if not for the blinding altar of golden statues. Another prime lesson from the ancestors: gaudiness to celebrate humility.

He scoffed at the notion, just as his father entered. Although Nobu was several years short of fifty, more salt than pepper topped his lean form. His Kyoto dialect reflected the gentleness of his eyes. He wore his usual *haori*, a twenty-year-old kimono jacket, simple and humble, the same as him.

'Good morning,' he said in Japanese.

Lane proceeded in his parents' language. 'Good morning, Father.' A slight bow sent his sunglasses down the irksomely low bridge of his nose. He nudged them upward to conceal his wound.

In the corner, his mother tended to the gramophone. Her song had ended, giving way to a loop of static. As she stored the record, his father settled on the couch across from Lane and absently rubbed dried glue off his thumb. Assembling his latest model airplane had tinted his fingernails red and blue.

Lane was tempted to kick-start the discussion, an acquired habit from his collegiate council position, but refrained. His family didn't operate as a democracy.

Finally, his mother moved to the couch and claimed her space. She folded her hands on her lap. Prim. Poised. A usual gap divided the couple, as if flanking an invisible guest.

'Your father would like to speak to you,' she prompted, a verbal tap of the gavel.

'Mmm,' his father agreed. He folded his arms and let out a deep exhale that stirred Lane's curiosity. 'It is the matchmaker in Japan. He has been working very hard for you, searching for a well-suited prospect.'

Shit, Lane thought, *not this again*.

He didn't realize the words had slipped out of his mouth until his father narrowed his eyes. 'Takeshi!' It was Lane's birth name, spoken with more surprise than anger.

Right away, Lane regretted not mirroring the respect his father had always shown him. 'I apologize. I didn't mean to say that.' *Only to think it.*

His mother tsked. 'You are in your father's house, not a dorm at your American university. If this is how you—' She stopped short. 'Remove your glasses when we are addressing you.'

For a moment, Lane had forgotten he was wearing them, and, more important, why. His mother's gaze bore through the lenses. Bracing himself, he unmasked his suddenly not-so-prideful mark, and his parents gasped in unison.

'What is this?' His father leaned toward him.

'It's nothing. Really. It looks worse than it is.'

'Nothing?' his mother said, incredulous, but his father continued on with concern.

'What happened? Were you robbed?'

'No, no,' Lane assured him. 'I was just at a club last night, when a brawl broke out.' Not the most tactful opening. Better to expound with highlights considered heroic in their culture; violence as a means of unconditional loyalty was, after all, a samurai staple. 'Some chump I went to Roosevelt High with was there. He was being disrespectful, not only toward me but against all Japanese. So' – better to keep things anonymous – 'a buddy of mine came to my defense. And when I tried to hold the bigger guy back—'

'Enough,' his father said. His eyes exhibited such disappointment, the remainder of the story stalled on Lane's tongue. 'I did not raise you to be a lowly street fighter. You have been afforded a better upbringing than that.'

Lane's mother turned to her husband. Shards of ice filled her voice. 'Did I not warn you? He is twenty-one years old, and because of you, he remains a child. All the idealistic views you have put into his head, to speak up when it suits him. As always, the nail that sticks out gets hammered down.' To punctuate the ancient adage, she flicked her hand to the side. The gesture effectively illustrated the quiet criticism she sent the man in every look, every day. An unyielding punishment, it seemed, for trading the dreams she'd once held for his. But his dreams were also for his children. Lane had always known this without being told.

Japan was a tiny island, crammed with farmers and fishermen and conformists, all bowing blindly to an emperor roosted on an outdated throne. Here, possibilities floated like confetti. Los Angeles was the city of angels, the heart of Hollywood, where imagination bloomed and promise hung from palm trees. Hope streamed in the sunlight.

America was their home, and Lane's need to defend that fact took over.

'There's nothing wrong with wanting to make a difference in this country. My country. *Emma's* country.' His delivery was gruffer than intended, but he wouldn't say 'sorry' this time. His sister, if no one else, deserved a safe place to plant the seeds of dreams and watch them grow.

Lane's father straightened. He rested his hands firmly on his spread knees in a contemplative, Buddha-like pose. Outside of his job, his greatest displays of strength were reserved for these kinds of moments. Moderating. Keeping the ground beneath their family level.

'Your mother is right,' he said evenly, and continued before Lane could argue. 'You are a man now. You must settle down. Carrying another's needs on your shoulders will focus you on your future.' In banking, he meant. A baby rattle made of an abacus had established the reference since Lane's birth. 'Therefore,' he added, 'we are pleased the matchmaker has found you a suitable bride, and he will make the necessary arrangements.'

Bride.

Arrangements.

The sentence replayed in Lane's mind, pulling him back to the original subject.

'She comes from noble lineage,' his father explained. 'The matchmaker has ruled out all the usual imperfections – tuberculosis, barrenness, and such. Her family's financial troubles make your pairing a sensible one. Her younger sister has found a match as well, so you must marry first. The family will sail over from Tokyo in time for the new year.'

'Hopefully,' his mother muttered, 'our son will look presentable by then.'

Lane scarcely registered the gouge. His mind was too consumed with the timetable his father had laid out. The rush of it all, the solidity. 'But – what about school? I still have a whole semester left.'

'She will live with us after the wedding,' his father said with a small nod to his wife, as if crediting the source of the solution. 'Once you graduate, you may make other plans if you wish.'

Lane's thoughts moved in a rapid tumble, blending into a mass of confusion. From that blur emerged a simple voice of reason. *Tell them the truth. Confess, as you've wanted to all along.*

Before he could reconsider, he tossed out his protest. 'I can't. I'm in love with somebody else.'

Tension of a new level swept through the room, conquering every inch of space. No one moved. No one spoke.

Lane wondered if anyone was breathing.

'You've met her before,' he said, easing them in. 'She grew up here, in Boyle Heights. She's a talented violinist. And she's charming and beautiful, responsible . . .'

'Her name?' Lane's mother spoke through lips that barely moved.

'Maddie.'

'Maddie,' she repeated as if judging the name by its taste, expecting a release of bitterness. The women had crossed paths on only a few occasions, during which his mother sustained disinterest. 'I do not know of this girl. Who is her family?'

First names meant little in their community; at least a third of the 'Nisei,' those born in America to Japanese immigrants, were called George or Mary. All significance lay in the surname, an indication of nobility, of lineage. Of race.

'If you mean Maddie's last name,' Lane hazarded to admit, 'it's Kern.'

His mother blanched. The lines spanning his father's brow deepened.

'She's TJ's sister,' Lane added, hoping their fondness of his friend would somehow permit a bending of their rules. Yet their scowls made clear there was no exception.

'You have made fools of us,' she hissed.

'Why? Because she's not Japanese?'

There was no reply. Which said everything.

'Father, you're the one who's so proud of your kids being American. That's half the reason you

33

came to this country. So why should it matter where Maddie's parents are from?'

Lane's mother patted her chest, grumbling under her breath, until her husband raised his hand, stilling her. His rigid words hovered above the quiet. 'The final decision has been made.'

A humorless laugh shot from Lane's throat. 'A decision I haven't been a part of.' He rose to his feet. 'Shouldn't I have a say in my own future?'

'This is not about you alone,' his father said, meeting his stance. 'This is about the honor you bring to your family.'

'What if I say no? What if I want to make my own choices?'

When his father hesitated, his mother supplied the answer from her seat. 'Then you will disgrace this family. And you will *not* be welcome in this home. Ever.'

Lane felt the stab of her tenacity, a knife between the ribs. He stared at his father in a desperate plea for support. Surely the man wouldn't be willing to disown his only son. Emotions aside, a male to carry on the name and bloodline was a fundamental basic.

'*Okāsan.*' Emma entered from the kitchen. 'I finished my breakfast. Can Lane and I go to the Pier now? Can we, can we?' Not receiving a response, Emma resorted to the parent whose soft spot for her was a reliable constant. 'Papa,' she begged, '*onegai.*'

Lane held his father's gaze for an eternal moment.

Every second sent a mixture of frustration and sorrow through his veins. He felt his limbs sag with each devastating pulse.

At the point of futility, Lane replaced his sunglasses. He would never look at his father the same. 'Get your shoes on, Em,' he told her. 'We're leaving.'

CHAPTER 5

The song had died. TJ scuffed his spikes on the mound, wishing for the life of him he could remember the tune. For all those high school shutouts and championships, an internal humming had carried him through. Its reliable rhythm had added a zip to any pitch from his hand.

Now, score tied at the bottom of the seventh inning, all he could hear was wind through the trees at Griffith Park and cheering from an adjacent winter-league ball game. Morning clouds soaked up any other sound.

The USC catcher flashed the sign. A curveball. TJ's old bread-and-butter.

A senior from St Mary's continued at the plate. He was a lanky walk-on TJ used to cream with fractional effort. Even sophomore year, just weeks after the holiday that had sledgehammered TJ's life, the guy couldn't compete. But that was before. Before TJ's world had turned silent and grim.

The hitter waggled his bat, waiting. Two balls, one strike, bases loaded with two out.

TJ tucked the ball into his glove. Worse than his sore jaw, a bone-deep ache throbbed from his knuckles. What the hell had he been thinking last night, throwing a right instead of a jab? Thankfully, Paul Lamont hadn't shown today, banged up as he must have been. It wouldn't have taken a genius to put two and two together, and the last thing TJ needed was the coach to think he'd become a hotheaded scrapper.

Blinking against the dusty breeze, TJ lowered his chin. He reared back with knee raised, adjusted the seams, and let the ball fly with a snap of the wrist. It broke low and away. A decent bend – just outside the strike zone.

'Ball!' the umpire declared.

Damn it.

TJ spat at the ground. He caught the return throw and tugged at the bill of his cap, blew out a breath. Gotta clear the melon. Start fresh without the clutter or a pitch didn't have a rookie's chance in hell. He loosened his neck, shook the stiffness from his hand. Strove to look calm.

The St Mary's batter smiled. He crowded the plate, his confidence growing.

But confidence could be a tricky thing. It lasted only if the person either had forgotten or didn't realize what they stood to lose.

TJ wished he had the leeway to send a reminder. Nothing like a knockdown pitch to wipe a smirk off a slugger's face.

Just then, the catcher tilted his head and shifted

his eyes toward the third-base foul line. It was a warning, understood in a game of silent signals. TJ glimpsed a figure he recognized in his periphery. Bill Essick was approaching their dugout. The Yankees' scout, a periodic spectator of Saturday league games, had once been a follower of TJ's career.

Time to turn up the heat.

The catcher appeared to understand. He pointed one finger down, a fastball high and inside.

TJ rose to his full height and grasped the ball in his glove. He paused, ears straining. Where was the song? *Where was it?*

In a pinch, he closed his eyes and forced himself to picture his father's face. On cue, anger boiled toward an eruption. Memories of the accident poured in a heated stream. The panic of tearing through the hospital halls, the police officer and his endless questions. The stench of the morgue, the lifting of the sheet.

He unshuttered his view and hurled the ball in a torrent – *smack* into the glove.

'Steee-riiike!'

Wiping his mind, TJ struggled to reduce his emotions to a simmer. He scuffed the mound again, hard.

Coach Barry nodded beside the dugout. A look of approval from the man, a praised coach of three sports for the Trojans, never lost its impact. He continued to be the major reason, in fact, that TJ attended University of Southern Cal.

But right now, Essick's opinion was all that mattered.

TJ rolled his shoulder muscles for the impromptu review. He could feel the scout's gaze on him. Just one more. All he needed was one more to smoke by the batter, one more to wrap up the inning. If he kept it up, he might even close out the game, from start to finish like the old days. Wouldn't that be swell.

The hitter set his stance. He gave home plate a little more space.

Catcher signed another fastball. It was a cocky choice though relatively safe, given the solid zip on the last pitch and drag on the swing.

Problem was, safe choices never led to greatness. Legends were made of risk takers armed with the skills destined for success. A display like that could be just the thing to regain Essick's interest, to see a winning thoroughbred in a stable of foals.

TJ grabbed hold of that risk, that sample of greatness, and shook off the catcher. 'Come on,' he murmured, 'something to dazzle 'em.'

The catcher complied: slider.

Now we're talkin', TJ thought. With a 3–2 count, the hitter wouldn't be expecting a pitch that chanced ending up out of the zone. And when done right, a slider gave the illusion of a fastball, up until it fell off a table the last several feet.

TJ readied for the windup. But just as he was about to close his eyes and dip once more into his cage of fury, a question snuck up on him: What if his rage soon tired of being locked up? He could feel its power increasing each time he let it loose to breathe and stretch. Brought out too often and that rage might end up refusing to go back in.

He squashed the thought and threw the ball with all the strength he could muster. Down the pipe it went. The seams spiraled away – a wall of wind seemed to slow every rotation – and laid tracks that led directly to the bat. *Crack*. The white pill soared overhead while the runners rounded the bases. Every footfall was a stomp to TJ's gut. Only for the mile-length arms of the left fielder did the ball not reach the ground.

The inning was over. TJ had pushed the batter to a full count and gotten the out, but once more he alone hadn't closed the deal. When it came to risks, the thinnest of lines separated a legend and a fool.

Quiet applause broke out while the USC players jogged toward the dugout. Following them in, TJ dared to seek Essick's reaction – not a total disaster; they were still tied, after all.

But the guy had already left.

CHAPTER 6

Apprehension reverberated through Maddie's body, a concerto plucking away the minutes. Inadvertently sticking her callused finger with another straight pin served as a reminder to concentrate on the job at hand. At least until Beatrice, the manager, arrived after a doctor's checkup. Then Maddie would be free to leave her father's tailor shop early, in order to present Lane with her decision.

She scooted her knees another few inches on the scarred wooden floor, dark as the paneled walls, and tacked up more hemline of the jacket. Emerald silk enwrapped Mrs Duchovny's robust form. A regular customer since Maddie's childhood, the woman had spent her youth as an opera singer. Her endless chatter in the full-length mirror evidenced her sustainable lung capacity. Even more amazing, she gesticulated as quickly as her lips moved, taking only tiny breaks to fluff her pecan-brown curls. None of this made marking her garments an easy task.

'Of course, you know more than anyone,' she was saying, 'I have enough holiday suits to clothe all of Boyle Heights. But with Donnie coming home on leave, I just wanted something special to wear for Christmas dinner. Especially after missing him over Thanksgiving. We only have three weeks to go, which doesn't give Bob much time. He's trying to surprise our Donnie with an entire wall of custom-made bookshelves in his room. That boy could read two books a day if he wanted. Did I ever tell you that?'

Maddie glanced up at the unexpected pause. 'I think you've mentioned it.' She pretended Mrs Duchovny hadn't already reported the same news about her Navy son a thousand times. Often Maddie wondered about the true reason the woman had insisted on becoming her benefactress for Juilliard. A charitable act of kindness? Or an investment in a potential bride for her son?

Mrs Duchovny prattled on, continuing to drop matchmaking hints, until Maddie announced, 'All finished.' Then Maddie snatched two stray pins from the floor and pressed them into the cushion bound to her wrist. She rose, wiping a dust mark from her apron.

'Madeline, dear.' Mrs Duchovny faced her, suddenly serious. The corners of her eyes crinkled behind her thick glasses. 'Are you feeling all right?'

And there it was. The dreaded question Maddie had heard more times than she cared to count.

'Yes, I'm fine. Thank you.' She forced a smile, feeling anything but fine, as always seemed the case when delivering the phrase. Fortunately, frequency of use had worn the roughness off the lie, turning it smooth as sea glass.

'Are you *sure* about that?' said Mrs Duchovny, resonant with disbelief. Before Maddie could repeat herself, the woman cracked a wide grin and displayed her right arm. 'Because I think you've forgotten a little something, dear.'

The other sleeve. Maddie had only tacked the left. 'Good grief, I'm so sorry.' She resumed her tucking and pinning as Mrs Duchovny chuckled.

'I'm actually relieved. For a minute, I was worried one arm had grown longer than the other.'

Maddie's lips curved into a full smile. Soon, though, she recalled her meeting with Lane. Today. At the Pier. And her anxiousness rose like the tide.

Oh, how she wanted to get the conversation over with.

She had planned to inscribe her thoughts in a letter, but just as she'd flipped over the *OPEN* sign this morning, Lane had phoned. He'd said he was headed to Santa Monica with his sister, and that he and Maddie needed to talk before he left town.

It's about us, he'd replied ominously when she asked if everything was all right. There had been a heaviness in his voice throughout the call, yet it was the word *us* that had landed with a thud, a trunk too burdensome to carry.

Clearly, he too had been pondering the impracticality of it all: A couple weeks for winter break and he would be back at Stanford; by summer's end, she could be off to New York for who knew how long. There would be no harm done should they simply put their relationship on hold, revert to friendship for now. If they were meant to be, destiny would reunite them.

The bell above the entry jarred Maddie back to the room. Beatrice Lovell entered – at last! – hugging a sack from the corner diner. It took two shoves for her to fully close the door. The sticking latch was among the list of repairs the seamstress had been chipping away at since becoming the shop's overseer.

Maddie hastened a review of Mrs Duchovny's sleeve lengths. Satisfied, she secured the second one with more pins.

'Lord 'a' mercy,' Bea exclaimed with her residual Louisianan accent. 'I thought I'd left hurricane weather behind me.' She set the paper bag on the counter. Outside the windows, red ribbons flapped on storefront wreaths. Passing pedestrians looked to the pavement, hats held to their heads in a tug-o-war with nature.

Mrs Duchovny clucked in response. 'I tell you, this wretched wind is a lady's enemy,' she said while Maddie eased her out of the jacket, guiding her around the exposed metal points. 'You should have seen the scattering of clothes that ended up in my backyard this morning off my neighbor's line. Good thing Daisy sews her name into her undergarments, because I wasn't about to go door-to-door in search of their owner.'

As Maddie hung up the coat, Bea dabbed two fingers on the tip of her tongue and tamed the silvery strands that had escaped her signature bun. Her pursed mouth created a coral embellishment on the wrinkled fabric of her skin. 'Brought us back an early lunch,' she told Maddie, and unloaded two wax paper–wrapped sandwiches.

Maddie opened her mouth to explain that she had a last-minute . . . well, errand to run. But Mrs Duchovny interjected, 'Ooh, I almost forgot. Donnie's favorite dress shirt is missing a button.' From a shopping bag near the sewing machines she produced a white, long-sleeve garb pin-striped in blue. 'I was hoping you might have one to match.'

'I'd be right surprised if we don't.' Bea turned to Maddie. 'Sugar, would you mind peeking in the back?'

Maddie strained to preserve her waning patience. How could she deny her patron a measly button?

'Not at all.' She accepted the shirt and hurried toward the storage room. Mothballs and memories scented the air, luring her inside, in every sense. It was here, between the racks of now dusty linens, that she and TJ used to hide, still as mice, awaiting a familiar waft. The fragrance of rose petals and baby powder. Their mother's perfume. A sign she'd returned from shopping at the market.

The giggling youngsters would huddle together as two sets of hands swooped in for the capture. And with their small bodies cradled in their parents' arms, a sound would flow through the air, lovelier than any sonata could ever be. For try as she might, Maddie had yet to hear a melody more glorious than their family's laughter. A four-part harmony never to be heard again.

Enough.

She wadded the thought, tossed it over her shoulder. There were plenty more where that came from, and the clock wasn't slowing. Lane, with a train to catch, would only be at the Pier another hour.

Refocusing, she scoured an old Easter basket filled with abandoned buttons, found a decent match, and headed down the hall. She was rounding the corner when she caught the women in hushed voices.

'Goodness me,' Mrs Duchovny lamented, 'I forgot how terrible the holidays must be for them.'

'Aw, now. You shouldn't feel bad, for having discussed your family gatherin'.'

'I suppose. Just such a shame, the poor girl.'

There was no doubt whom they'd been talking about. The same family everyone was always talking about. After two years of rampant whispers, Maddie should have been used to this.

Bea popped her head up with an awkward abruptness. 'Any luck, sugar?'

Maddie swallowed around the pride, the voiceless scream, lodged in her throat. 'I found a button that'll work.'

'Splendid,' Mrs Duchovny gushed, her cheeks gone pink. With arms appearing weighted by guilt – or pity – she reached out for the items.

'No.' Maddie stepped back, her reply a bit sharp. She held the shirt to her middle and softened the moment with a smile. 'That is, I'd be happy to do it for you. No charge.' She would have offered normally anyhow, yet it was her sudden inability to unclench her hands that left her without choice.

Mrs Duchovny conceded, followed by a rare moment of quiet. 'I'd best be getting home. Bob will be sending out a search party soon.' She shrugged into her fur-collared overcoat and covered her locks with a brimmed hat.

'We'll call y'all when everything's ready,' Bea said, and ushered her to the exit while they exchanged good-byes. A burst of air charged through before the door closed, rocking Maddie onto her heels. And not for the first time, she was surprised to discover she was still standing.

CHAPTER 7

'Kern!' Coach Barry's voice shot over the departing spectators at Griffith Park. 'Need a word with you, son.'

TJ fought a scowl as he zipped up his sports bag. Since being pulled for the last two innings, he'd been counting down the minutes to leave. Their closing pitcher had held on for a 7–5 victory, but TJ wasn't in the mood to celebrate.

He slung his bag over his left shoulder and hid his purpling bruises by dangling his right hand behind him. Thankfully, only a muted yellow tinted his cheek.

Coach Barry strolled toward the outfield, a signal for TJ to join him. A private talk. Not a good thing, considering TJ's mediocre showing today. The solid, dark Irishman carried a thoughtful look, hands in the pockets of his baseball jacket. A taunting wind blew past them. It flapped a lock of the man's slicked hair, receding from the effects of close-call games and concern for his players.

As they passed the pitcher's mound, TJ mined his brain for arguments to defend himself. He wasn't about to surrender all hope of regaining his slot in the starting rotation for USC's upcoming season. When his game had gone to hell last year, a compassionate demotion landed him in the bullpen. Now he wanted out. He was a prisoner who knew what it was like on the other side of the fence, and could feel his cell closing in on him. Telling the coach about a new pitch he was honing might aid his cause. A 'slurve,' they called it. The slider-curve combo could break wide enough to raise some brows.

He was about to volunteer as much when Coach Barry asked, 'So how's your father been?'

Your father.

Swell. Was there anything TJ wanted to talk about less?

'The same,' he answered. Which meant mute in a convalescent home, nearly too depressed to function.

Coach Barry nodded pensively. 'I'm sorry to hear that.'

TJ squeezed the strap on his bag. Redirecting, he said, 'My sister, Maddie, though – she's doing great. Her violin teacher says she's a shoo-in for Juilliard this year, if her audition goes well. Just gotta keep her on track till then.'

'That's good, that's good.' Coach Barry smiled. 'I'm sure you've done a fine job looking out for her.'

TJ shrugged, despite feeling as though caring for Maddie was the one thing he was still doing right.

'What about you, son? How you doing these days?'

'I'm gettin' by.' The reply was so reflexive, he didn't consider the bleakness of the phrase until it was too late to reel the words back in. ''Course, if you're talking about baseball, I can assure you, my pitches are coming back more and more every day. You just wait and see. By spring practice—'

Coach Barry held up his hand, bringing them to a stop. 'Look,' he sighed. 'I'm gonna cut to the chase. Your professor, Dr Nelson, paid a visit to my office last week. It's about your grades.'

The path of the conversation, in an instant, became clear. A detour TJ resented. He didn't need their sympathy, or to be ganged up on. That woman had no business stirring up trouble on the field.

'It was a couple lousy tests,' he burst out. 'I've told her that. Got plenty of time to make it up.'

'And the rest of your classes?' The challenge indicated Coach Barry was well informed of the situation. That his former-ace pitcher was barely skimming by, tiptoeing on the fence of a scholarship lost.

TJ clenched his jaw. He wrestled down his anger, to prevent it from seizing control.

Coach Barry rested a hand on TJ's shoulder, causing a slight flinch. 'I know you've been through a lot, son. But you've got less than a year left, and I, for one, don't want to see you throw it all away. Now, if you need a tutor, you just say so. Or if you need more time for studying, we can certainly see about cutting back your delivery hours. . . .'

Less time dedicated to his on-campus job was a nice thought, particularly on days of lugging cadavers from Norwalk State Hospital for the Science Department. Yet a nice thought was all it was. Besides school expenses, TJ needed all the dough he could get for house bills and Maddie's lessons and everything else in the goddamned world that chomped its way through a pocketbook.

'I'll be fine, Coach,' he broke in. He repeated himself, taking care to stress his gratitude. 'Really, I'll be fine.' If it hadn't been for the guy's encouragement, TJ would have dropped out of college long before now.

Coach Barry rubbed the cleft in his chin before he heaved a resigning breath. 'All right, then. You know where to find me.'

TJ obliged with a nod. He remained on the faded lines of the diamond as his coach walked away and disappeared from sight. At that moment, in the wide vacancy of the ball field, TJ suddenly realized why he had always been a pitcher.

Because alone on the mound, he depended only on himself.

CHAPTER 8

Maddie stood on the Pier, searching, searching. Though unbuttoned, her long russet coat hoarded heat from her anxious rush across town. A current of strangers split around her like a river evading a rock. An ordinary rock, medium in size, nearly invisible. And Maddie preferred it that way. Only when channeling another's composition through her bow did she now find comfort in the spotlight.

Scanning faces, she hunted for Lane's distinct features, his sister's pint-sized frame. Outside the Hippodrome was where he had asked Maddie to meet them. But they weren't there, and she didn't have the luxury of time to wait patiently. It was a quarter after noon. She had but fifteen minutes to spare. He couldn't have left early; she'd told him she would be here as soon as she could. She needed to find him, before he left, before his train.

Before she lost her nerve.

'Lane, where are you?' At the very moment she whispered the words, she spotted the back of his familiar form blinking between passersby.

His golden skin peeked out between his short black hair and the collar of his coat.

She prepared herself while striding over the wooden planks to reach him. 'I'm so glad you're still here,' she said, touching his arm. He turned toward her, revealing the face of a man with sharp Italian features. Mustard stained his large lips.

'Pardon me,' Maddie said. 'I thought you were somebody else.' Then she streamed into the mass, head down. Blending.

The smell of onions from a hot-dog stand caused her stomach to growl. In her haste, she'd left the lunch Bea had insisted she take for the bus ride over. Macaroni salad and a baked-bean sandwich. Maddie had grown to love both as a child, long before she could comprehend which meals were served solely to survive the shop's less-profitable months.

But she couldn't think about any of that now. She had ten minutes to find –

'Maddie . . .'

She focused on the vague call of her name, filtering out the crowd's chatter. Notes of 'In the Mood,' from the band on a nearby stage, took greater effort to block; music dominated her hearing above all else.

'Maddie!' At last, the soprano voice guided her to Emma's china-doll face. The girl was scurrying toward her with a smile that made perfect little balls of her rosy cheeks. Maddie used to secretly babysit her when Lane was in high school. Naturally, he had preferred outings with TJ over watching his pesky little sister. He'd been adamant about paying by the hour, though Maddie would have done it for free. And one look at the youngster reminded her why.

'Hiya, pretty girl.'

Emma leapt into her outstretched arms. Adoration seemed to flow from the child's every pore. It filled Maddie's heart so quickly she had to giggle to prevent her eyes from tearing up.

As their arms released, she noted a substance on Emma's hands. 'Ooh, you're sticky. Let me guess, cotton candy?'

'*And* a caramel apple,' Emma boasted. Then her smile dropped. 'Don't tell my mom, okay?'

'My lips are sealed.' An easy promise to make. Running into the woman, unreadable in her stoicism, had always occurred by mere chance, and Maddie's talk with Lane would do anything but change that. 'Say, Emma, where's your brother?'

Emma twisted to her side and pointed. There was Lane, weaving around a family ordering ice-cream cones. He wore a trench coat and sunglasses. A bright red balloon floated on a string clutched in his hand. When Maddie caught his attention, he flashed a smile, the breathtaking one that seemed crafted just for her. She felt a warm glow rise within her.

'I was getting worried,' he said, once they were close.

'Sorry it took so long. We had customers, so I couldn't leave until Bea showed up.'

Emma tugged her brother's sleeve, looking troubled. 'I thought you were gonna get yellow?'

Lane glanced at the inflatable swaying overhead, as though he'd forgotten it was there. He squatted to her level. 'Turns out they were out, kiddo. But since Sarah Mae's favorite color is red, I was hoping this would do.'

Emma contemplated that, and nodded. 'Good idea. Sarah Mae loves balloons.'

Maddie smiled at the reference to the girl's doll, equally ragged and beloved, while Lane tied the string around his sister's wrist.

'*Onīsan*, can we go down to the sand?' Emma asked him. 'I didn't get to collect shells yet.'

The Japanese term for 'brother' was one of the few things Maddie understood about Lane's foreign culture.

He checked his watch. 'I guess we can. We only have a few minutes, though, so don't go far. And don't wade too deep into the water.'

'Okay, okay.'

'You promise?' he pressed.

Emma sighed, her pinkie drawing an *x* over her chest. 'Cross my heart,' she said, and rolled her eyes, not in rebellious defiance, but in a gentle manner. As if at the age of eight, she could already see his barriers for what they were. An expression of caring. It wasn't so different, Maddie supposed, from the strict guidelines TJ had instilled after assuming their father's role.

Except that she herself wasn't eight.

Side by side, Lane and Maddie walked toward the beach. Strangers with rolled-up pants and buckets and shovels speckled the sandy canvas. A choir of seagulls cawed as they circled yachts in the harbor, muting the hollers of a teenage boy chasing a scampering black puppy. The dog was yipping toward a pair of brilliant kites dancing in the air. With attentive eyes, Lane watched his sister sprinting like the pup, bobbing beneath her flag of a red balloon.

The picture of him as a father hit Maddie with a swell of emotion she swiftly shoved into a box, stored away for the future.

'How's your eye?' she asked.

He shrugged, half a smile on his lips. 'It's still there.'

'Could I see?' Noting his reluctance, she added, 'I'm sure it's not as bad as you think.'

Slowly, he reached for the glasses and slid them free. In the swollen bruising she discovered an irony of beauty she didn't expect. He'd always projected such certainty in her uncertain world that strangely she found the sight comforting, proof of his vulnerable side. A symbol of commonality she could actually touch.

'Does it hurt?' Her fingertips brushed his skin before she could remind herself to keep her distance.

'It'll heal.'

She nodded and withdrew her hand. Her gaze shifted to the distant figure of Emma, whose raised arms couldn't reach her fleeing balloon. Already twenty feet up, it zigzagged a path toward the ceiling of clouds, away from the chaos, the worries of life. Maddie had the sudden desire to be tethered to its string.

'I don't have much time,' he said. 'But we need to talk. . . . It's about us.'

That phrase again.

He gestured to a thick, weather-beaten log. 'Why don't we sit down?'

She didn't reply, simply led them to perch on the bumpy seat. Waves before them lapped the sand, weakening the shore layer by layer. She clasped her hands on her skirted lap. So close to Lane now, she could almost taste the fragrance of his skin. It smelled of citrus and cinnamon and leaves. At the Pico Drive-in, where they'd spent numerous dates necking through double features, Maddie would inhale that lovely mixture. Afterward, she'd sleep in the cardigan she had worn, to savor his scent until it faded.

Would their memories together just as surely disappear?

She banished the thought. She needed to concentrate, to review the practical reasons to loosen their ties. Their usual outings, for one: hidden from crowds, cloaked in darkness. Lookout points and desolate parks. Only on occasion would they venture to the openness of a bowling alley or skating rink, requiring them to refrain from acts of affection.

Just like now.

Lane hooked his glasses in the V of his royal-blue sweater. He stared straight ahead as he continued. 'Last spring, you told me you thought it was best if we didn't tell anyone about our dating, and I went along with it. I lied when I said I agreed.' He wet his lips, took a breath. 'But the truth is, you were right. It was better that we didn't say anything. My family wouldn't have understood, what with our . . . differences. God knows, they wouldn't have taken us seriously. They might have even thought I went steady with you to make a point.'

Their racial diversity had, before now, seemed an off-limit topic. An issue to deny through tiptoeing and silence. But more striking than this new candidness was his usage of the past tense. *Went steady with you. Wouldn't have taken us seriously.*

He wasn't asking for her opinion. To him, the relationship was already over.

'I'm tired of sneaking around,' he said. 'I don't want to lie anymore. I don't want *you* to lie anymore. Especially to TJ. He's more than a friend, he's like a brother to me.'

She couldn't argue. None of this had been fair, to any of them.

'Maddie . . .' Lane's mouth opened slightly and held. He seemed to be awaiting the arrival of a rehearsed conclusion, a finale to their courtship. He angled toward her with a graveness that wrenched her heart. 'There's something you don't know. Something I should've told you before, but I wasn't sure how.'

Maddie blinked. What was he talking about? What had he been keeping from her?

'It's my parents,' he said. 'They've arranged a marriage for me.'

The word *marriage* entered her ears with a calmness that, in seconds, gained the piercing shock of a siren. 'To whom?' she found herself asking.

He scrunched his forehead, a revelation playing over his face. 'I'm not sure, actually. The *baishakunin* – the matchmaker – found her in Japan. Tokyo, I think they said. Anyway, her family is supposed to be a good fit.'

'I . . . didn't realize . . . they still did that.' The response was ridiculous, trite. Yet the blow was too great to formulate anything better.

'The custom is crazy, I know. But as their oldest son, their only son, it's my responsibility to do what's best for the family.' Annoyance projected in the timbre of his voice. He shook his head. 'It's no more than a business negotiation. Same as my parents were. And they want to bring her over right away.'

A scrapbook materialized in Maddie's mind: a portrait of Lane in a tuxedo, beside him a wife as exotic as her wedding garb; their children waving to the procession of a Chinese New Year parade; a snapshot of the family at Sunday supper, a foursome with identical almond eyes.

'All of this,' he said finally, 'is why I needed to

see you.' He laid his hand on hers, a sympathetic gesture. 'I've given it a lot of thought, and there's only one thing that makes sense for us.'

The breeze blew a lock of her hair that caught in her eyelashes, a shield to hide her welling tears. She lowered her lids and waited for the words: *to break up.* She'd been foolish, so foolish to believe she could walk away unscathed.

'Maddie,' she heard him say. 'Will you marry me?'

Once the question fully soaked in, her eyes shot open.

'What?'

He smiled. 'Marry me.'

She couldn't answer. Her thoughts were a jumble of fragments. An orchestra of musicians, each playing a different piece.

Lane brushed the strands from her face and tucked them behind her ear. He tipped his chin down, peering into her eyes. 'The only way they'll ever accept us is to not give them an option. Maddie, I love you. I want to see you every morning when I wake up, and fall asleep every night next to you. I want us to raise a family and spend our whole lives together. And if you feel the same' – he tenderly tightened his grasp on her hand – 'then marry me.'

Logic. She grappled for any shred of logic. 'We can't though. It's – not even legal here.' A fact she'd known yet never liked to dwell upon.

'Just the wedding isn't. The marriage would be

perfectly valid. A college friend of mine is from Seattle. He says interracial couples get married there every day.'

'Seattle?'

'That's right,' he said. Then his smile faded into something tentative. 'But sweetheart . . . we have to do it next weekend.'

Next weekend? *Next weekend?*

The very idea was rash, and insane. She tried to protest, yet her sentence amounted to a whisper. 'That's so soon.'

'There's no other choice. They plan to bring the girl's family here before New Year's. I don't want to hurt other people, just because we've waited too long.' He caressed her cheek. 'I know we're meant to be together. Since the first time I kissed you, I've known it with everything in me.'

The warmth of his fingers on her face revived the memory of that day. He'd been there when she came home from visiting her father, another one-sided exchange. Lane had been in town for the weekend, relaxing on their couch while TJ finished up at the ball field. She'd walked in to find a fresh envelope from the Juilliard School of Music. Even though she'd predicted their decision – a surety after her poor audition – reading the actual form rejection had struck her with a reality that ripped through the seams of her soul. The reality of lost dreams, a lost life she had taken for granted.

Until then, she had been proud of how dignified

she'd been about it all. The perfect portrayal of strength in the face of disaster. But with the weight of that letter in her hands, dignity became too much to carry. When her strength buckled, Lane was the person who'd caught her. She literally cried on his shoulder, soaked his shirt with pent-up grief. He held her close and safe, stroked her hair. And once their lips joined, more than passion flowed through her; it was the peace of finding someone whose heart felt tailor-made to match hers alone.

Now, with Lane's hand on her cheek, her skin melting into his palm, she felt the same over-whelming emotion. The family she'd been raised in was gone, but she and Lane could start a family of their own. The kind she'd always dreamed of. Together, they could be happy.

'Yes,' she answered.

'Yes?' A request for clarity.

'Yes.' She smiled. 'I'll marry you.'

Recognition settled in his eyes and a grin across his face. He jumped to his feet and drew her up into his arms. Their hearts were pumping at the same rapid pace. 'Oh, Maddie, I love you so much,' he said against her temple.

'I love you too,' she whispered. She had conveyed the sentiment plenty of times, on notes she'd snuck into his pockets, or in letters she'd mailed to Stanford. Yet only now did she become aware of how much she meant the words.

He leaned back and gazed at her, his eyes glinting

with joy. Then he placed his curled fingers under her chin to bring her in for a kiss. Their mouths were a few inches apart when a voice cracked through the moment.

'*Onīsan*,' Emma yelled. 'I found one!'

In an instant, they stood a respectable distance apart, though Maddie couldn't say who had created the gap. How could she have forgotten where they were? That Emma, too, could have been watching?

'Look!' The girl ran toward them, holding up something round and white. 'It's a whole sand dollar. And it's not broken or chipped or anything. It's a sign of good luck, right?'

Lane gave Maddie a brief glance and grinned again. 'Definitely.'

'Did you know there's five doves inside?' Emma asked Maddie. 'And the North Star is in the middle, and an Easter lily's around it?'

Unable to speak, Maddie nodded.

'Wow.' Emma studied the shell. 'I can't wait to show Papa. He's gonna love it. Can we go home and show him? Can we?'

Lane looked at his watch, then sighed. 'I guess we'd better go. My train . . .'

'Of course,' Maddie said, regaining her voice.

He turned to his sister. 'Hey, Em. Race you to the snack stand?' He didn't have to ask twice. She automatically assumed a runner's starting pose. 'Ready?' he called out. 'Set . . . go!'

Unlike Emma, Lane didn't dash away. He

stepped back toward Maddie and, picking up from where he left off, he leaned in and placed his lips on hers. Although she closed her eyes, she saw a vision of strangers walking past, pointing, whispering their disapproval. And when the kiss ended, she couldn't help feeling relieved.

'See you next Saturday?' he asked.

She prodded herself to nod.

'You promise?'

'Cross my heart,' she said lightly, pushing out a smile.

He touched her check once more, then jogged off to catch up to his sister. After the two faded into the crowd, Maddie lowered herself onto the log. A chill from the wind prickled her neck. She crossed her arms and stared out into the endless ocean that stretched straight up into the clouds.

Remembering Emma's balloon, she panned the sky for what had become a tiny red dot. When it vanished from sight, she wondered how much pressure she, too, could take before bursting into nothing.

CHAPTER 9

'Got any idea what you're lookin' for?'

TJ turned from the hardware store's shelves to find his sister's friend Jo. Her tone made clear she doubted he could find the right part on his own. Just the kind of conversation he needed after the lecture from his coach.

'I got it handled.' He swung his attention back to the bins of gaskets, the same ones he'd been staring at for the past five minutes. The smells of kerosene and turpentine were making him light-headed, compounding his frustration.

'Problem with the sink?'

He edged out a nod.

'Kitchen or bathroom?'

'Kitchen,' he muttered, picking up a random gasket to study the thing. He was hoping she'd take her cue to move on to another customer roving her family's store.

But she didn't. She continued to watch him, hands in the pockets of her gray work uniform. Her lips bowed in amusement. 'You know, I could save you a whole lotta time if you let me help.'

Was there a skywriter over his head today announcing he needed charity?

He snapped his eyes to hers. 'I said I got it.'

Pink spread over her cheeks, a look of surprise, then aggravation. 'Suit yourself.' She pivoted sharply on the heel of her loafer. By the time she exited the aisle, TJ saw himself for the jerk he'd been.

'Shit.' He flung the gasket into the bin. Abandoning his sports bag on the cement floor, he trudged after her, ready to smooth the waters with the *I'm-just-tired-and-have-a-lot-on-my-mind* spiel. Sure it was only half the story, but no one needed to hear more. He rounded the corner and bumped a display of paint cans. The pyramid held its ground. Jo's loose ponytail in his sights, he trailed toward the cashier's table in front. He was about to call Jo's name when a voice from the side stopped him cold.

'TJ,' was all she needed to say and he knew it was Cindy Newman.

The harsh fluorescent lights did nothing to take away from her stunning face, her knockout figure. The girl was known to pass as Veronica Lake any day of the week, and today was no exception. Her golden hair draped long and styled, her sundress snug around the curves. Her full lips shimmered in the same red that had tainted his shirt collars more than once.

'Hi, Cindy.'

She smiled broadly. 'How have you been?'

'Doin' all right. You?'

'Terrific, thanks.' The difference between their answers was that hers sounded genuine. 'So,' she said after a pause, 'who won?'

It took him a moment to follow the question. He'd forgotten he was wearing his baseball uniform and jacket. He wished he could as easily forget about the game. 'We did.'

'That's grand. You were pitching?'

'Yeah.' He left it at that.

'Then I'm not surprised.' She offered another smile, though this one wasn't solid enough to block the awkwardness rising between them. She fidgeted with her purse handle and glanced down and away. It was the same look she'd given at the end of their last date, a look that said she didn't expect to hear from him again. No question, she had put in effort. She'd tried to talk to him, to kiss him until he would open up. But his wall of fury had sealed her out.

He realized now, more than a year later, that he'd never explained that to Cindy. Never told her it was nothing she'd done.

A grizzled man in overalls wandered past with a shovel, the cash register rang out a sale, and TJ decided another place would be more appropriate for this conversation. 'You know, maybe, sometime,' he said, 'if you're not busy—'

Jo's brother Wes was marching in TJ's direction. The oldest of the five Allister boys, he'd been a quiet but popular linebacker. Latest word had it

67

he was on a winning streak of boxing matches around the city. A guy you didn't want to piss off by insulting his sister.

TJ was about to speak up but didn't make it that far. Wes took the first shot – by scooping Cindy up by her waist. 'There you are,' he said, and nuzzled her neck, inducing a giggle.

'Were you worried I'd gotten lost?' she teased.

Wes gazed at her with pure adoration, oblivious to any others' existence. 'I'm all finished here with inventory. How about a movie at the Palace?'

She groaned. 'Is there any picture we *haven't* seen this month?'

He held her close and whispered in her ear, prompting more giggles, her face to blush. TJ did his best to pry away his focus. He felt intrusive, irritated, regretful. And yeah, jealous. Not of being with Cindy necessarily. Just of any guy who could truly be that happy.

The couple headed for the door. As her boyfriend held it open for her, Cindy angled back. An after-thought. 'It was good seeing you, TJ. You take care.'

He nodded, staring after her. She'd moved on, as she should have. She was better off with someone who had his head on straight.

'Anything I can help you with, sonny?' From behind the counter, old man Allister regarded him over the rims of his bifocals.

Jo touched the man's shoulder. 'It's all right, Gramps. He's not one who takes kindly to help.' After flicking TJ a cool look, she pushed through the swinging half-doors of the storage room. It was then that TJ recalled why he'd trailed her through the store. Yet the urge to follow her was gone.

CHAPTER 10

Lane wasn't aware his mind had been wandering until something hit him in the forehead. He jolted back in his cushioned leather chair. A wad of notebook paper had landed on his leg. He could guess the culprit before looking up.

'At least we know he's alive.' Dewey Owens smirked at the other two guys in their study group before turning to Lane. 'I was getting worried that punch had bruised more than your eye.'

Lane pitched the crumpled ball right back. But with Dewey's eagle eyes, a match to his beak-like nose, he ducked in plenty of time.

'Have to be faster than that!'

A student in the corner of the common room sent a curt, 'Shhh,' to which Dewey retorted, 'Relax, bookworm. Finals ain't till next week.' No doubt, he'd thrown out the grammatical error just to grate on the stuffy kid's nerves; Dewey had been born to a wealthy L.A. family, same as Lane. Both saddled with the tedium of properness.

'So where were we?' Lane flipped forward in his economics book. Envisioning his rendezvous with Maddie wasn't going to speed up the week. 'Did we already cover the graph on page one-o-one?'

Dewey reclined with feet on the coffee table and addressed the classmate beside him. 'Gotta love my roommate. Almost four years now, he's been pretending to cram just for my sake. Bastard aces his classes without even trying.'

'That's not true,' Lane said.

'Oh?'

'I try. A little.'

Dewey laughed. 'Imagine what you could do if you were actually interested in your major.'

Lane had imagined it all too often, and to no point. Political Science wasn't an option according to his family's conditional funding. In contrast, Dewey's Economics degree – using numbers merely to support the conceptual and theoretical – would serve as a small rebellion against his father, the owner of an accounting firm.

'Lane Moritomo in here?' some guy called out.

'Yeah, that's me!'

'Girl's on the phone for you.'

Fighting a grin, Lane set aside his book. He had been hoping all afternoon that Maddie would ring him back once her brother left the house. 'That's gotta be my sister,' he told his study pals.

'Pass along my thanks,' Dewey said, 'for making those paper birds.' The origami cranes were what he meant, folded by Emma's tiny hands to bring them luck on their exams.

'Sure thing.' It drove Lane crazy not being straight with his roommate.

Soon that would change.

At the phone in the hall, Lane brought the handset to his ear. A pair of athletes in Cardinal sweatshirts strolled into the dorm. For privacy, he spoke just above a whisper. 'Maddie?'

'Am I speaking with Lane Moritomo?' It was indeed a woman, but he didn't recognize the voice.

'Uh, yes. This is Lane.'

'Mr Moritomo, this is Congressman Egan's office.'

'Yes?' he said again, thrown off guard.

'Sir, I'm phoning to inform you that you've been chosen for an internship.'

Her sentence lit a fuse. It traveled through him, gaining potency and speed, until he exploded with excitement. 'I can't believe it! My God – I mean, my gosh.' A small circle of students glanced over. Lane cranked his volume down. 'I . . . don't know what to say.'

'How about, you accept the offer?' A smile broke through her businesslike tone.

'Of course. I definitely accept.'

'Congressman Egan will be delighted to hear that. Your enthusiasm and fresh ideas made quite an impression.' Lane strove to listen, despite his yearning to scream while sprinting through every corner of the Quad, around Lake Lagunita and back. 'You'll receive more details by post, but feel free to contact us with any concerns. Otherwise, we look forward to seeing you in June.'

'Details. In June.' Thoughts tumbling, he barely remembered to add, 'Thank you, ma'am. For letting me know.'

'My pleasure.'

The line went dead, but Lane was afraid to release the handset, as though the phone were his sole link to the internship.

Among all the politicians in the region, Egan most closely shared his visions of equality and civil rights, community outreach. Of immigration and landowning laws needing to be reformed. Ongoing peace talks between Japan and the U.S. were dandy, but why stop there? Increasing American commerce in the East would benefit everyone.

To each of Lane's points, the congressman had listened, and concurred. Egan maintained that the government existed to serve the public, not the other way around. He was a doer, not a talker. And somehow, Lane's foot had managed to wedge into that esteemed man's door.

Granted, it was only an internship and the pay wouldn't be much, but it was a stepping-stone toward a brighter future. A future he couldn't wait to share with Maddie.

Maddie. She was the first person he wanted to tell.

The operator connected the call. He started tapping his thumb on the phone after the first ring. By the fourth, it felt like forty.

'Kern's Tailoring.'

He was so thankful Maddie had answered he plunged straight in. 'The internship. At the congressman's office. Sweetheart, I got it. I got it!'

'Wow, that's wonderful,' she said. 'I'm so proud of you.'

'I thought I had a good shot, after the interview, but . . . there were so many applicants—' He heard Maddie talking to someone, her voice muffled from covering the mouthpiece. 'Maddie?' He waited. 'Honey?'

'Sorry, I'm here. And I do want to hear more, but there's a whole wedding party being fitted.'

He squelched a budding of disappointment. 'No problem.'

'I'm happy for you, though. Truly I am.'

'It's fine, I understand,' he assured her, then remembered the upcoming weekend. 'Besides, I can tell you more in person, when we meet on Saturday.'

'Oh, right. Saturday,' she agreed. But there was a catch in her voice that tugged like a hook in his chest. He was about to investigate the cause when the reason became clear.

Egan's office was in California; Juilliard was in New York.

'Don't worry about this affecting your schooling, okay? We'll figure it out, no matter what.'

Muffled again, she spoke to a customer, then, 'Sorry, Lane, I have to run. Talk to you soon.'

'Okay then, take care. I—' *Click.* 'Love you.'

The hallway went eerily quiet.

By the time he hung up the phone, he chose to brush away his senseless worries. There was too much to celebrate. The internship of his dreams, a key to his future, had been dropped into his hands. Maybe there was magic in those lucky cranes after all.

He sped to the commons and shared the news with Dewey, who demanded they toast at Danny Mac's Pub to commemorate the triumph.

Later, once the elation and beer began to wear off, they crashed in a happy stupor on their beds. And that's how Lane remained until late that night, when he awoke from a nightmare, sweat beading his face. The scene imprinted in his mind left him unable to sleep: At Seattle's Union Station, he stood on a platform, awaiting his future bride – who never showed.

CHAPTER 11

Dreariness hung in the air, rivaling the pungency of medications and disinfectant. The odors, however, didn't bother Maddie. With each visit to the convalescent home, her nose had grown more tolerant of the strange, sterile surroundings, as had the rest of her senses. The sight of elderly residents struggling to feed themselves over-boiled food, or getting agitated at relatives they no longer recognized, had gradually lost its impact. Even glimpsing shriveled bodies holed up in their beds, disguised chariots headed for the afterlife, caused Maddie only occasional pause.

She pondered this while rosining her bow, preparing for her performance. As she stood alone in her father's assigned room, it dawned on her how accustomed she had become to the bland, beige walls and scuffed tiled floors, the clusters of wheelchairs and muted floral paintings. A sadness rose within her.

He wasn't supposed to be here this long.

The doctor had recommended a change in scenery to help cure his depression, some place free from the memories of his wife. Beatrice Lovell had been quick to highlight the amenities of the rest home owned by her husband, as if selling a vacation house on the Malibu shore. Of course, more than the vastly discounted rate communicated her unspoken favor. Given that Maddie and her brother had both been in school, and lacked any close relatives, Bea had secured the care their father needed. Perhaps even rescued him from an asylum.

What else did authorities do with people whose grief stripped their desire to function?

'Mr Kern, look who's here,' a nurse encouraged. She guided him into the room in a slow shuffle.

'Hi, Daddy.' Maddie dredged up a smile, held it as his glassy blue eyes panned past her face. The routine persisted in delivering a sting.

Before the window, the nurse eased him into a chair. He angled his face toward the glass pane. 'Your daughter's going to play for you today. Won't that be nice?'

Holiday garland swagged above him. The fading afternoon light bent around his slumped shoulders. For an instant, time reversed. It was early Christmas morning. He wore his bathrobe over his pin-striped pajamas, his brown hair disheveled. Bags lined his eyes not from aging sorrow, but from a late night of assembling Maddie's new dollhouse, or TJ's bicycle for the paper route. Maddie could still see her dad settling on the davenport, winking at his wife as she handed him a cup of strong black coffee. Nutmeg and pine fragranced a day that should have lasted forever.

'If you need anything, I'll be at the desk,' the nurse said to Maddie, doling out a smile. The pity in the woman's eyes lingered in the small, stark room even after her departure.

Maddie shook off the condolence and retrieved the violin from her case. She methodically tuned the strings. Photographed composers stared from the lid, always in judgment.

Today, theirs wasn't the approval she sought.

She took her position before the music sheets. Each lay in sequence side by side on her father's bed. Height-wise, the pages weren't ideally located, but she knew the composition forward and backward. The wrinkled papers, strewn with penciled finger markings, merely served as a security blanket.

'I've been working on a Paganini caprice for you. His ninth, one of your favorites.'

He didn't respond, not so much as a blink.

She reminded herself that the title alone would carry little impact.

As she nestled the violin between her chin and collarbone, she played the opening in her mind. There was no room for error. The perfection in her phrases, her aptness of intonation, would wake him from his solitary slumber. Lured out of his cave and back into their world, he would raise his eyes and see her again.

She lifted the bow, ticking away two-four time

in her head. Her shoulder ached from relentless practices. Scales and arpeggios and fingered octaves had provided escape from gnawing doubts over her looming nuptials.

If only life could be as well ordered as music.

Maddie closed her eyes, paced her breathing, and sent the bow into motion. The beginning measures passed with the airiness of a folk dance in a gilded palace, where women with powdered unsmiling faces and tall white wigs tiptoed around their buckle-shoed partners. Soon, the imitative notes of a flute alternated with dominant horn-like chords, and after a brief rest, the strength of the strings pushed through an aggressive middle section. Maddie's fingers leapt up and down the fingerboard. The bound horsehairs hastened through ricochets and over trills. Any ending seemed miles away until a soft high-B floated on melodic wings. Only then did the prim courtiers return. They lent their limelight to a ruler's abrupt pronouncement, before trading bows and gentle curtsies. When the final note drifted away, Maddie opened her eyes.

Her father's seated form appeared in blurred lines. As they solidified, her anxiety climbed the hill molded of hope and dread. Her technicality had been pristine, a rendering her instructor would deem 'admirably spotless.'

But had she chosen the right piece? The right composer?

Violin held snug to her chest, she watched and

waited for the answers. In the silence, her father inched his face toward hers. A trembling of antici-pation spread through her. Their gazes were about to connect when an unexpected sound robbed her focus. At the door a matronly nurse stood behind a woman in a wheelchair, pit-patting their applause.

Maddie jerked back to her father – whose atten-tion had returned to the window. His expression remained as dispassionate as those of the composers in her case. Once again she stood before him, alone and unseen. She'd become the beige walls, the tiled floor. An insignificant fixture he passed in the hall.

She sank down onto the bottom corner of his bed. Instrument resting beside her, she leaned toward him. 'Daddy, it's me . . . Maddie. I know you can hear me.'

At least she hoped so. Even more today than usual.

Suddenly she recalled her impromptu audience. She glanced at the empty doorway before contin-uing. 'Since my visit last week, some things have happened. You see, the thing is that Lane – the Lane you've known for years – well, he proposed to me. In a couple days, we're supposed to get married.'

For a second, she envisioned her father shooting to his feet, outraged she had accepted without his consent, a sure sign he'd heard her.

He didn't react.

'I love Lane, I honestly do. It's just happening

80

so fast. We've only been dating since the spring, and he's been away half the time at school. Then there's Juilliard, and now he's got a job offer in California . . . I'm not sure of anything anymore. And even if I were, how can I do any of this without you?' She went to touch his hand, but reconsidered. Grasping fingers that made no effort in return would crumble the strength she'd rebuilt, day after day, note by note.

Maddie tightened her grip on her violin, growing more insistent. 'You're supposed to walk me down the aisle. You're supposed to tell me what a good choice I've made, and that we're going to live happily ever after.' The impossibility of it all brought tears to her eyes. 'Please, Daddy,' she urged in a whisper, 'talk to me.'

He continued to stare out the glass. He didn't utter a sound.

Her answer, however, came regardless. From a cavern of truths, it echoed from deep inside. All she had to do was listen.

CHAPTER 12

Hunched over the kitchen table, TJ attacked the page with a vengeance. He scrubbed at his lead markings with a pencil eraser, but the layered numbers still peeked through. Five layers to be exact. That's how many times he'd been stumped by the blasted stats equation.

Such a waste. Waste of an evening, wasted effort. Baseball had already taught him all the math he ever wanted to use. Measurements from the mound to every point of the plate, the trajectory of hits, angles of pitches, addition of runs, the subtraction of players.

He'd chosen Business as his major. It seemed the least specific option. In actuality, a degree was never part of the plan. His vision of the future had been nothing but stripes. Not of the flag, a symbol of patriotic roles meant for guys like Lane. No, his own allegiance lay with the good ol' Yankees, with those dapper stripes, their top-notch talent. And TJ's name could have been – should have been – added to their roster long before now.

Freshman year, only one teammate besides himself had been recruited on scholarship. The second baseman, a fellow All City player, signed last year with the Red Sox. Yet here was TJ, still stuck in Boyle Heights, trying to rid his life of another mistake that couldn't be wiped clean.

Although that didn't keep him from trying.

Rubber shavings scattered as he wore down the eraser at an angle. When the nub snapped off, the pencil's top skidded across the paper. The metal rim tore a rut through the single problem he'd actually gotten right.

He chucked the pencil across the room. Growling, he crumpled the page. 'Stupid, useless piece of—' He reared back to pitch the wad, but a discovery halted him.

Company.

At the entry of the kitchen, Jo Allister leaned against the door-jamb. Her oversized peacoat hung open around her overalls. 'Don't let me interrupt,' she said. A baseball cap shaded her face, though not her bemusement.

'Don't you ever knock?'

Her mood instantly clouded. 'I'm looking for Maddie. If that's acceptable to you.'

This made for the second time this week he'd misdirected a vent on his sister's friend. He surrendered the balled paper onto the table, tried his best for a nicer tone. 'She's not here.'

Jo upturned her palm as if to say, *You wanna elaborate?*

'She . . . went to see our dad.' Based on periodic reports from the nurses, any visits were pointless.

Maddie just hadn't accepted that yet. 'Afraid I don't know when she'll be back.'

'Fine. Then tell her I swung by.' With a scathing smile, Jo added, 'I'd stay and wait, but you might take up throwing knives next.'

Once again, he watched her ponytail shake with fuming steps away from him. She certainly had a knack for jumping straight into his line of fire.

'Hold on,' he called out weakly. Her shoulder flinched, indicating she'd heard him, but she didn't stop.

He marched after her. 'It wasn't you, okay?'

Ignoring him, she opened the front door. He caught hold of her sleeve.

'Jo, please.'

She didn't face him, but her feet held.

'I just got a lot on my plate, with baseball and finals and . . . everything.'

Gradually she wheeled around. Her bronze eyes gave him a once-over. 'That supposed to be an apology?'

TJ found himself without a response. He had lost the skill of presenting a proper sorry. It was tangled up in the net of regrets that a million apologies couldn't change.

'You're welcome to stay' – he gestured behind him – 'if you wanna wait for Maddie.' Padding the peace offering, he told her, 'No knife throwing, I swear.'

A reluctant smile lifted a corner of her mouth.

She glanced past him and into the house, considering. 'I dunno.'

Man, was she going to make him crawl over hot coals for her forgiveness?

'Looks like we've both been cooped up too much,' she said. 'Come on.' She waved a hand to usher him down the steps.

He had to admit, it was a nice night. From the smells of leaves burning and cookies baking next door, he sensed his stress dissolving, making her offer tempting. Still, he felt the tug of obligation, recalled the equations that weren't going to solve themselves.

'Stop your fretting,' Jo said. 'Your books aren't gonna run off. Or your pencil – wherever it landed.'

He gave in to a smile. 'All right, all right. Let me grab a jacket.'

TJ glued his gaze to the asphalt to avoid the lineup of houses they passed. It wasn't the string of gingerbread cutouts that made him want to scream, but the normalcy.

Middle class to upper class, nearly every ethnicity peppered the neighborhood – Russians, Mexicans, Jews, you name it. The families' after-supper scenes, however, varied little. Fathers smoked their pipes, slippered feet crossed at the ankles, reading newspapers or books, or playing chess with a son eager to turn the tide. Mothers in aprons tended to children all bundled in nightclothes; they double-checked homework or darned socks beside the radio; they nodded to the beat of a youngster plunking away at a piano. Some even had the gall to hang Christmas decorations – December had scarcely arrived!

TJ was so intent on blocking out these lousy Norman Rockwell sketches, he didn't give any thought to destination until Jo spoke up.

'This is it.' She jerked her thumb toward the sandlot.

'This is what?'

She rolled her eyes, making him wish he'd just played along. 'You know, TJ, you're about as good at apologizing as you are at listenin'.' She continued into the ballpark, collecting rocks from the lumpy dirt.

TJ slogged behind. By the light of the moon, he took inventory of the place he hadn't visited in at least a decade. The park was even more run-down than he remembered, and smaller. A lot smaller. When the new ball field had opened several blocks away, complete with kelly-green grass and shiny cages and splinter-less benches, kids had immediately shunned the old hangout. It was a toy they'd outgrown and dumped in a dusty attic.

Only now did TJ detect a sadness etched like wrinkles in the sandlot's shadows.

'Right over there.' Jo pointed out a set of sagging bleachers. 'That's where I carved my initials, front row on the left. My own VIP seat. Every weekend Pop and I would come here and watch my brothers play. I tell ya, we missed a heap of Sunday Masses, but never a Saturday game.' She jiggled the rocks in her hand as if seasoned at throwing dice. Even TJ would think twice before going up against her in back-alley craps. 'One day the coach got so tired of me nagging about wanting to hit, he put me in. Thought it would shut me up.'

'Well, obviously *that* didn't work.'

Without warning, she flung a pebble that TJ barely dodged.

'And that, buster, was with my left arm.'

TJ shook his head. A quiet laugh shot from his mouth as he dared to follow her.

On the sorry excuse of a mound, level as the Sierra Madres, Jo planted her loafer-clad feet. A pitcher's stance. She transferred the rocks, save for one, into her coat pocket. With her right hand, she drew back and slung the stone at her target, the lid of a soup can dangling from the batter's cage. *Plunk.* The tin rattled against the warped and rusted fence.

Not bad. For a girl.

'So, how'd you make out?' he asked. 'Up at bat?'

'Walked,' she said with disdain. 'A beanball to the leg.' She flipped her cap backward with a sharp tug and set her shoulders. Sent out another nugget. *Plunk.* 'My brother Otis was pitching. Told his buddies he wanted to teach me a lesson, which was baloney. He was terrified of his little sister scoring a home run off him.' She wound up and threw at the lid again, as hard as her expression. Another bull's-eye. Three for three. Without daylight.

TJ tried to look unimpressed. 'How long ago all this happen?'

'I dunno. Eight, maybe nine years back.'

A smirk stretched his lips. 'And . . . you're still holding a grudge?'

She pondered this briefly, rubbing a fourth stone with her thumb. 'Irish blood,' she concluded. 'Forgiving wasn't exactly passed down by our ancestors.'

TJ, too, had a dash of Irish mixed into his hodge-podge of European descent. Perhaps this explained his shallow well of forgiveness. He dreaded to think what other traits he'd inherited from his father.

Averting the thought, he focused on the road that had delivered them there. 'I gotta get back.'

'No,' Jo said.

He turned to her. 'No?'

'Not till I show you why I brought you here.' She tossed her rock aside and sat on the mound. Then she slapped the dirt beside her twice, peering at him expectantly.

He scrunched his face. 'Um, yeah. As nice as it would be to hang out and tell ghost stories, I do need to get some studying done.' His future at the university sadly depended on it.

'Two minutes and we'll go.'

'Jo, I really need—'

'Would you stop your moanin' and take a load off?'

Clearly arguing would get him nowhere. And he couldn't very well leave a girl, no matter how self-reliant, alone at night in a deserted park. Safety aside, it was just plain rude.

'All right,' he muttered, 'but make it quick.' He took a seat on the packed slope.

'That wasn't so hard now, was it? Now, lie back.'

'What?'

She groaned at him. 'Just do it.'

Concerned by her intentions, he didn't move. The two of them had never really hit it off, but if any other girl had invited him to cozy up like this, he'd know where it was leading.

'Don't flatter yourself,' she spat as if reading his thoughts. Then she lay back, head on her hands, convincing him to recline.

The coolness of the ground soaked through his clothing, sparking a shudder. 'Now what?'

'Relax.' She took a leisurely breath. 'And look up.'

He cushioned his neck with his fist and dragged his gaze toward the sky. The lens of his vision adjusted, intensifying the spray of white specks. Clear as salt crystals on an endless black table. Were the stars tonight brighter than usual? Or had it simply been that long since he'd paid notice?

Within seconds, everything else faded away. He was suspended in space, floating among those specks like he'd dreamed of as a kid. He was an adventurer visiting other galaxies, a fearless explorer. There were no responsibilities anchoring him in place. And for the first time since he could remember, TJ felt free.

'This is what I wanted to show you.' Jo's voice, like gravity, yanked him back to earth. Again, he lay in the old ballpark. 'My pop,' she went on, 'he knew everything about the stars. Was a big hobby for him. He's the one who taught me about constellations making up pictures and whatnot.'

'Yeah?' TJ said. 'Like what?'

She gave him a skeptical side-glance. Seeming satisfied by his sincerity, she raised her arm and pointed. 'You see those three running up and down in a row?' She waited for him to respond.

'I see 'em.'

'Well, they're the belt hanging on Orion, the hunter. And next to it, right there, are three more dots that make the line of his sword.' She picked up speed while motioning from one area to the next. 'Above him is Taurus, that's the bull he's fighting, and on the left are his guard dogs. The lower one is Canis Major, and the star at the top of it is Sirius. That's the brightest star in the night sky. Believe it or not, it's almost twice as bright as the next brightest star. . . .' Not until she trailed off and cut to his gaze did he realize he was staring at her. 'Swell.' She looked away. 'Now you think I'm a nut job.'

'Actually, I was thinking . . .' He was thinking that he'd never noticed what a pretty face she had. Had a naturalness about her. She wasn't one for wearing makeup, and he sort of liked that – though he wasn't about to say it. 'I was wondering how you remember so much about all of them. The constellations, I mean.'

'Oh. Well. I don't remember them *all*. Those are just some of my favorites.'

'What's so special about them? Compared to the others?'

She lifted a shoulder, signs of embarrassment having fallen away. 'I like that they have a whole story. Plus, you can see them from anywhere in the world. It's kinda nice, don't you think? Some stranger in a faraway country's gotta be looking at those very shapes right now.'

Jo turned back to the sky, and after a beat, she quietly added, 'Mostly, though, I guess they remind me of my dad. I like to think of him as Sirius, the brightest one. Way up there, watching over me and my brothers.'

Normally TJ would bolt from a moment like this, averse to poking and prodding, yet he felt compelled to hear more. 'What exactly happened to your parents?'

'Depends. Which version you lookin' for?'

He understood the dry response. The local rumor mill had churned out plenty of whoppers about his own family, so he didn't give much credence to anything he'd heard about Jo's. When she and her brothers moved into town, to live with their granddad, stories had spread like wildfire. Some claimed her mother ran off with another guy, supposedly a traveling missionary from Canada; others said friendly fire took out her father during the Great War. TJ could have asked Maddie for the real dope, after the girls met in junior high, but he hadn't considered it any of his business.

Probably still wasn't.

He decided to nix his question, but then Jo up and answered.

'Plain truth is, my ma died while giving birth to my brother Sidney. I was only two, so I don't remember much about her, outside her photo. As for Pop . . . on the dock where he was working, some wire on a crane broke loose. A load of metal pipes dropped. Folks said he pushed another fella outta the way and that's why he bought it. Wanna know the screwy thing? It wasn't even his shift. He was filling in for another guy who'd come down with the flu.' A sad smile crossed her lips. But then she heaved a sigh, and the moisture coating her eyes seemed to evaporate at will. 'Just goes to show you. Of the things we're able to control, death sure ain't one of them.'

'Pffft, right.' The remark slipped out.

Jo angled her face toward his. She hesitated before asking, 'You wanna talk about it? About your parents?' The glow of the moon highlighted a softness in her features. She looked at him with such profound understanding that he genuinely felt the relief of someone sharing his burden.

The cost of the moment, however, was remembering.

Suddenly that horrific night, usually flashing in pieces, stacked like a solid wall of bricks. He closed his eyes and the emergency room flew up around him. His father lay in a hospital bed, forehead and shoulder bandaged, gauze spotted with blood. Bourbon oozing from his pores.

Once he's conscious, we'll need him for questioning, the policeman said. There was an accusation in his voice. When TJ's mind stopped spinning, he found himself in the passenger seat of the officer's car. Rain hammered the roof as they drove through the streets, shrouded in darkness. With every passing headlight, he saw his father's sedan winding down the canyon road, colliding with the oncoming truck. He imagined the spontaneous sculpture of bloodied bodies and twisted metal, saw the New Year's Eve party the couple had left only minutes before the accident.

Cars honked in ignorant celebration as TJ mounted the steps to the morgue. Round and round 'Auld Lang Syne' played in his head as the coroner pulled back the sheet – *Should old acquaintance be forgot* – and TJ nodded once in confirmation. If not for her gray pallor, the absence of breath, his mother could have been sleeping. A doctor arrived to identify the other driver, a widower lacking a family member to do the honors. *We'll drink a cup of kindness yet . . .* TJ drifted out the doors. He thought of Maddie, and the task of telling her the news when she returned full of laughter and tales from her group holiday concert in San Francisco.

It had been at that moment, outside the morgue with drizzle burning cold down his face, that TJ swore two things: He would protect his sister at all costs; and he would never, for anything in the world, forgive his father for what he did.

'Maybe it would help,' Jo said, 'if you talked about it.' The tender encouragement opened TJ's eyes. 'I know it helped me an awful lot when I finally did that with Gramps.'

A sense of comfort washed over TJ, and he couldn't deny wanting to purge the memories. But how could he put those images into words? And how could Jo truly relate? Her dad was a hero; his own, a murderer. Sure, an inconclusive investigation had prevented any charges – whether it was the truck driver or his father who'd crossed the median, whether booze or the slick road was to blame.

Yet to TJ, the key evidence lay in his father's reclusion and, more than that, his inability to look his children in the eye.

Jo kept watching, in wait of an answer.

'Another time,' he said, almost believing it himself.

She twisted her lips and nodded thoughtfully.

Rising to his feet, he extended a hand to help her up. She dusted off the back of her overalls, her peacoat. 'Home?' she asked.

'Home,' he replied, the word sounding distant and hollow.

CHAPTER 13

The morning crept by, chained at the ankles. Lane stole another glimpse at his watch. *Don't worry*, he told himself. *She'll be here. She'll be here.*

For three nights in a row, the same scenario had plagued his dreams. Clear as the aqua sky now overhead – unique weather for a Seattle winter, according to passersby – he had visualized himself in this very spot. On a platform at Union Station, waiting futilely for his fiancée's arrival.

To quell his concerns, he had contemplated phoning her again from his dorm. Yet calling without warning meant the possibility of reaching TJ or Beatrice and raising unwanted suspicions. Thankfully the charade would soon be over. At last he could tell her brother the truth – presuming cold feet hadn't kept Maddie from boarding her train.

Although Lane tried to dismiss it, he'd sensed her uncertainty, both at the beach and on the phone. And how could he blame her? A sudden rush to the altar should rightly cause reservations. He just hoped her love for him would be powerful enough to conquer any doubts.

Excited murmurs swirled. A train appeared in the distance, chuffing on tracks that led toward Lane. An eternity bloomed, then wilted, before the dusty locomotive chugged to a standstill. A cloud of steam shot out like an exhale of relief, of which he felt none.

He bounced his heel on the weather-stained concrete, hands fidgeting in his trench coat pockets. Minutes later, passengers poured from the coaches. Men in suits and fedoras, ladies in coats and brimmed hats. Lane's gaze sifted through the commotion. Families and friends reunited. Children squealed, set free to release their bundled energy. At a faraway glance, he mistook a lady for Maddie, clarified when the stranger angled in his direction. He rose up on the balls of his feet for a better view. But still no sign of her.

Lane confirmed with the conductor that this was the overnighter from Los Angeles – both good and poor news. Could she have missed her train, taken another?

The likelihood of the more obvious taking hold, dread rushed through him. Somehow only with Maddie at his side did defying his parents make sense. Fighting the muzzle that would bind his future to a stranger would require, while hopefully only temporary, a break from his family. Without a strong incentive, rebellion would be hard to justify. Even to himself.

Once more, Lane reviewed the train cars. The

crowd was thinning, hope growing sparse. What was he to do now?

He started toward the station's Great Hall, needing to regroup, to process, until a sight ensnared him.

Maddie . . .

In a burgundy suit jacket and skirt, she lugged a suitcase down the steps of the lead coach. Sunlight added radiance to her creamy skin, her swaying auburn hair. She spotted Lane and sent an enthusiastic wave.

Grinning, he hastened to meet her. He picked her up and held her close, savoring the fragrance of her jasmine perfume. It flowed like her music into his heart. That's where he'd stored every note she had played at her last performance. Her movements had been so entrancing; if not for Jo nudging him to applaud, he'd have forgotten that TJ, or anyone else in the audience, was there.

'Gosh, I'm so sorry you had to wait.' She spoke with a lingering panic as he set her down. 'I almost missed my connection, so I didn't have time to check my baggage. Which was fine, until the darn latch caught on a seat while I was carrying it off and my clothes scattered all over the aisle. People offered to help, but I just couldn't accept. My undergarments and nightdress were in there and . . .' She put a gloved hand to her face. 'Good grief, I'm rambling, aren't I?'

He rubbed her blushing cheek with his thumb and shook his head. 'You're perfect.'

When she smiled, he drew her in for a kiss. Her lips tasted of mint, their texture like Japanese silk. But even more wondrous, he sensed a new comfort in her display of affection. From the discovery came an instant desire to sweep her off to their hotel. It was an urge he would have followed if not for the importance of one other stop.

He pulled his head back and Maddie slowly opened her eyes. 'So, Miss Kern,' he said as though suggesting an afternoon stroll, 'how would you feel about tying the knot today?'

A knock announced the message: It was time.

'I'll be right out,' Maddie called to the closed door. She finished smoothing her hair in the tall oval mirror and straightened her suit jacket. Dust motes danced like fireflies in the spill of light through the window. A four-poster bed, two Victorian chairs, and a square table with a bowl of peppermint candies filled the makeshift dressing room, leaving little space for her nerves to jump and jitter.

Another rap sounded on the door.

What was the hurry? There weren't any other couples when they arrived here, a minister's residence on the outskirts of the city. A few more minutes to prepare for this momentous step seemed reasonable enough.

On the other hand, eliminating time to dwell would be wise. Little good would come of imagining the very different wedding she had pictured as a child, with the smashing gown and mile-long veil, the church pews teeming with friends. And most of all, her mother's sweet fussing, her father's arm to guide her.

'May I?' Lane asked, poking his head in.

'Of course.'

Inside, he shut the door with his heel. Approaching her, he paused and tilted his head in concern. 'Is something wrong?'

Pondering her parents must have left clues in her expression – signs Lane could mistake for second thoughts on marriage. 'I just thought it was bad luck,' she said quickly, 'seeing each other before the wedding.'

'I didn't think you believed in old wives' tales.'

'Better to play it safe, don't you think?' In truth, she didn't want to taint their day with mentions of past sorrows. 'Honey, you need to go. The ceremony will be starting.'

'Without us?' His eyes gleamed. 'Now, pick a hand.'

Until then, she hadn't noticed he held his arms behind his back. 'What is it?'

'Pick a hand,' he repeated.

Neither of his bent elbows gave a hint. 'I don't know. This one.' She tapped his right shoulder. He flashed an empty palm.

'Now which one?'

'Lane,' she grumbled.

He laughed softly before presenting her the gift. A bundle of peach roses, each bud a flourish of perfection. White ribbons bound the thorn-less stems.

'Can't be a bride without a bouquet,' he told her.

She barely deciphered his words. The flowers in her hand, their reminiscent color and scent, pinned her focus. 'These roses,' she breathed, 'they were . . .'

'Your mom's favorite,' he finished when her voice faltered.

She nodded, amazed he had logged away such a detail.

'And let me tell you' – he smiled – 'they weren't the easiest things to find in Seattle in December.' Growing more serious, he moved her hair off her collar. His fingers brushed past the side of her neck. 'But I thought you might want something of your mother with you today.'

The bittersweet sentiment tightened Maddie's throat, just as he added, 'I've got one more thing for you.'

What could possibly top what he had given her?

To her surprise, he went to the door and signaled to someone in the next room. The recorded notes of a solo violin entered the air with a slight crackle. Bach's Chaconne. It was the final movement of his Second Partita, by far among his grandest works. Which was why Maddie's father used to listen to it on their phonograph so often. Somehow the piece had slipped through her repertoire.

She felt moisture gather in her eyes, unaware a tear had fallen until Lane returned to her and wiped it away. 'Thank you,' she said, unable to verbalize the scale of what the presents meant to her. She leaned in for a kiss, but he gently put a finger to her lips.

'Not yet,' he whispered.

Maddie beamed in agreement, remembering the impending ceremony. Then a revelation struck. 'Oh, no.'

'What's wrong?'

'I didn't give *you* anything.'

'Yeah, you did,' he replied, confusing her. 'You said yes.'

Such power lay in a single syllable. *Yes.* Scarcely a word, a reverse gasp really, it was an answer capable of forever altering the landscape of a person's life. And yet, to Lane's proposal of marriage, she would say it a hundred times over.

'I'll be in the other room,' he said. 'Come out whenever you're ready.'

Once he'd left, she brought the bouquet to her nose. At the old fragrance of home, she recalled a memory of Lane and her family. A slow month at her dad's shop had elevated nerves while they awaited a scholarship offer for TJ. A rise in the cost of Maddie's lessons clearly hadn't helped. Seated at supper, each Kern drifted so far into thought, no one realized Lane had built a tower of biscuits twelve layers high. Maddie was the first to notice his attempt to crack the tension. He gave her a knowing wink, a secret traded between them. By the time her family caught on and all broke into smiles, something small but deep in her had changed. In a single look, she'd finally seen Lane as more than her brother's friend.

She held on to that moment now, a scene of the two of them surrounded by her family's joy. It wasn't hard to do, thanks to the gifts Lane had given – her mother's favorite scent, her father's beloved notes. She drank them in as she opened the door and headed for the aisle.

In what appeared to be a dining room, lacking a table to hinder the cozy space, she walked in time to the Chaconne; its harmonic middle section resembled a church-like hymn. A stained-glass cross glowed red, blue, and gold in the window. The watercolor of light projected a kaleidoscope over her open-toed heels, guiding her to Lane. Beside him, the Methodist minister waited, wrinkled as the leather Bible in his hand. The man's wife looked on in delight from the corner, where she supervised the Victrola.

Bach continued to roll out the carpet of chords. Once Maddie turned to face Lane, the music miraculously faded from her mind, as did everything in the room but him. Lost in his eyes, she listened as he vowed to love, honor, and cherish her. In kind, she devoted herself through good times and bad, through sickness and health, till death would they part. She embraced him as their lips met, sealing her heart and name: Mrs Madeline Louise Moritomo.

★   ★   ★

The day unfolded with more enchantment than Maddie had imagined possible.

Never one to break a promise, Lane had handled every detail from the marriage license to the rings, gold bands perfect in their simplicity. She wasn't a fan of jewelry that would impede her playing, and he'd understood this without being told. He understood everything about her.

For their first night as newlyweds, Lane had reserved a hotel room downtown. The accommodations were going to be nice, he'd said. Nice. His tone was one Bea would use to describe a Mint Julep or Mrs Duchovny's son. Perhaps a little girl's party dress with bells sewn into the petticoat. *Nice* didn't come close to describing their gilded suite.

If not for Lane carrying Maddie over the threshold, she might have fainted in the marble entry. *Splat.* There went the bride.

What a story that would have made for the bellboy behind them balancing their luggage. As Lane directed the placement of their belongings, Maddie explored the lavish furnishings. Copper-hued satin draped from the ceiling in a waterfall of luxury over an enormous bed. Claw-footed chairs flanked an oversized window. At the center of the framed view, a burnished sun slid behind a train station. The building had inarguably been modeled after the Campanile di San Marco. In high school, she had studied the famed bell tower of Italy. The redbrick structure boasted an arched belfry, a pyramidal spire, and a cube displaying images of lions and the female symbol of Venice, La Giustizia. *Justice.*

Somehow, a time machine had zapped Maddie into the drawing room of Giovanni Gabrieli. No wonder the Venetian composer had contributed such significant works to the High Renaissance. With a view like this, motets and madrigals must have flowed like water from his quill.

'What do you think?' Lane's arms looped her waist from behind. 'Not a shabby way to kick off a marriage, huh?'

Rooted back in reality, she noticed the bellboy was gone. She and Lane were alone. In a room where all barriers would soon be removed, her nervousness strummed.

'It's marvelous here,' she said, gently breaking away. She retreated to the curtains, projecting a fascination with the embossed ivy and fleur-de-lis pattern. 'Are you sure we shouldn't go someplace else, though? This must be costing a fortune.'

'Well,' he drew out. 'It does help that I secretly rob banks for a living. Including my father's.'

She kept her eyes on the fabric and felt him getting closer. 'Really, Lane, I didn't expect all this extravagance.'

Right behind her again, he stroked the back of her hair. Each strand tingled as he offered a level explanation. 'When I was in high school, my father put some funds in the bank for me, a nice start for after college. Of course, you and I will have to find a modest home at first. But that'll change, once my internship turns into more. Or I'll find an even better opportunity near Juilliard.'

It suddenly hit her that she hadn't considered any details past their nuptials – where or how they would live, before and after his graduation. Everything had happened with the force and urgency of a tornado. Besides thoughts of her father, the sole concern crouching in the back of her consciousness had been her brother.

As far as TJ knew, she was traveling with Jo to visit the Allisters' cousins in Sacramento for the weekend. To cover her bases, she'd told Jo she would be away for a performance. This time, more than any other, she'd despised fibbing. She just couldn't jeopardize complicating her decision with others' opinions. Better to ease them into the news once all was solidified.

Lane turned her around with care. 'All of that,' he said, 'we can talk about later. This is our wedding night, and I don't want you to worry about anything.' He pressed her hand to his chest. 'Just know, I'm going to take care of you, Maddie. So long as we're together, the rest will work out.'

The assertion cradled her, as solid and real as the throbbing of his heart. With every beat, the trust he had nurtured expanded, pressing down her defenses.

She linked her hands behind his neck and brought him to her. Lane trailed kisses across her cheek, into the curve of her neck. A soft moan escaped her. No longer would they hide in the darkness of a drive-in, shadowed by worries of who might see. From the freedom they'd been granted – in the eyes of God and the law – she yearned to be closer than ever before.

Sensibility, nonetheless, reminded her to do this right. She forced herself to pull away from the magnetism of his hold. 'I'd better freshen up,' she rasped.

He paused before yielding a nod, his breathing heavy.

Regaining her composure, she slipped into the bathroom fit for a palace. Steam crawled up the mirrors as water filled the porcelain tub. She unboxed a bar of honey-milk soap and, when the bath was ready, twisted off the faucets. In the vaporous space dripping with gold and marble, she removed her clothes, then remembered. She'd left her nightgown in her suitcase.

Drat.

A problem, yes, but easily remedied. She threw on a plush hotel robe from the door hook. To fetch her garment, she would sprint both to and from her luggage. That was the plan, anyhow, until she stepped into the room, its fabric-lined walls aglow with candles on the nightstand.

'Thirsty?' Lane's voice came gently from the side, inches from her ear. The smell of champagne sweetened his breath. Candlelight flickered over his bare chest and down the muscles of his stomach. At the sight of his pajama pants, relief battled disappointment, her curiosity swelling.

She ignored the flute of champagne in his hand and ran her fingers along the contours of his shoulders. For years, while he and TJ played basketball at the park, she had witnessed a younger, leaner version of this very chest, these same arms. She'd pumped away on the swings, on a pendulum in her own universe. That girl had no inkling that one day the touch of his skin would ignite passion that stole her breath.

Lane set aside his glass and led her to the bed. When he lowered her onto the cream comforter, billowy with down, she closed her eyes. His fingers traced the collar of her robe and edged the fabric away from her body. Her breasts prickled from a tepid draft of air. Her mind grew dizzy approaching the act she knew little about, outside scandalous passages from a book Jo once swiped from beneath an older brother's mattress.

'My nightdress,' Maddie murmured, recalling her mission.

Sensing his movements had stopped, she lifted her lids and discovered him gazing at her, his head propped on an elbow. A tender smile crinkled the skin bordering his eyes. 'I don't think you'll need it,' he said. 'But if you're saying you want to slow down . . .'

The compassion in his voice soothed her unease, drawing her into another dimension like she'd thought only music could. She rose up and placed her mouth on his. Their bodies soon discovered a natural rhythm, and all reservations fell into an abyss. For it was here, safe in the heat of his arms, Maddie came to believe anything was possible. The rest of the world be damned.

Like their night of lovemaking, waking up next to Maddie – his *wife* – surpassed any expectation. Lane never wanted to leave the surreal bubble encasing them. Only from the incessant grumbling of his stomach did he agree to her suggestion that they venture out for a meal. It was, after all, almost noon.

With her arm hooked snugly around his, they emerged from the hotel. Once a block down, he pointed to a restaurant across the street. 'That's the one.'

'Let me guess,' she said. 'It's the fanciest diner in town.'

'Nope. Just the closest. I'm starving.'

She laughed. 'Oh, and whose fault is that?'

He whispered in her ear, 'I'm happy to take the blame. Last night was worth it.'

'*And* this morning,' she reminded him.

Her growing brazenness made him want to flip around and head straight back to their hotel room.

They'd make it a quick meal.

Inside the diner, the aroma of bacon caused his stomach to complain yet again. He led her to an empty booth by the window. The seats were easy to nab with so many customers clustered around a radio on the counter. Too late in the year to be listening to the play-by-play of a Rainiers game. The announcer must have been relating the latest of FDR's policies. When else would a crackling transistor warrant this much attention?

Usually, Lane would join in, craving every word from the President's mouth. But not today. 'I'm ready to order when you are.'

'Hold your horses,' she said, grabbing a menu from behind the napkin dispenser. 'Let me see what they have at least.'

'Better make it snappy, 'cause my belly isn't about to wait.'

'Jeez. What happened to chivalry? You *are* my husband now, aren't you?'

'Hey, I swore to love and cherish. Never said anything about putting you before hunger.'

Mouth agape, she batted at his forearm, and they broke into laughter. When they settled into smiles, he clasped her fingers. She stared at their interwoven hands.

'Why do we have to go back to California?' she sighed. 'Why can't we just stay here?'

Lane mulled over the idea. It wasn't impossible. He had plenty in savings to afford a couple more nights of heaven. 'Who says we can't?'

'Yeah, sure.'

'I don't have exams till Friday. And you said there's nothing you have to rush home for.'

She studied him. 'You're serious.'

'What's stopping us?'

'Well . . . I told TJ I'd be back tomorrow. . . .'

'So, you'll send him a telegram and let him know you're staying a few more days.'

She hesitated, taking the suggestion in. 'I guess I could. But – I didn't pack many clothes.'

He leaned forward and answered in a hushed tone. 'Mark my words. I'll make sure you don't need any of them.'

Her eyes widened, looking embarrassed. Then a giggle won out.

'Well, what do you say, Mrs Moritomo?' His finger rested on her wedding band. 'Want to treat this like a real honeymoon?'

She bit her lip, her cheeks still blushing. At last she nodded in earnest.

'Good.' He grinned. 'Now, let's eat, so we can hurry back to the room.' He twisted around to find a waitress and muttered, 'Isn't anyone working here?'

Through the dozen or so people gathered across the room, Lane spied flashes of pastel-blue diner dresses behind the counter. He waved his hand to no avail. The gals were too far away for a polite holler. Rising, he groaned before his gut could beat him to it.

'I'll go get someone,' he told Maddie. As he moved closer to the group, mumbles gained clarity.

'Dear God.'

'How many were there?'

'What does this mean?'

He sidled up to a bearded stranger in back of the bunch. A faded denim shirt labeled the man approachable. 'What's going on?' Lane asked.

The guy answered without turning. 'We been bombed,' he said in a daze of disbelief. 'They've finally gone and done it.'

'*Bombed?* What are you talking about? Where?'

'Hawaii. They blasted our Navy clear outta the water.' The man shook his head. 'We're going to war, all right. No way around it.'

'But who?' Lane demanded. 'Who did it?'

The guy angled toward Lane, mouth opening to reply, but he suddenly stopped. His eyes sharpened with anger that seemed to restore his awareness. 'You oughta know,' he seethed. 'Your people are the ones who attacked.'

The train's whistle stretched out in the tone of an accusation. Once the locomotive had cleared the claustrophobia of Seattle's looming buildings, Maddie forced her gaze up. *The Saturday Evening Post* lay limply on her lap. She'd absorbed nothing of the articles. Their print, like the universe, had blurred into smears of confusion.

She scanned the coach without moving her head. Her neck had become an over-tightened bow. Her wide-brimmed, tan-colored hat served as an accessory of concealment. Suspicious glares, however, targeted the suited man beside her: Lane, who hadn't spoken a word since leaving the hotel. Lane, who could always be counted on for a smile. A guy who could conjure solutions like Aces from a magician's sleeve.

Lane, her *husband*. The word hadn't yet anchored

in Maddie's mind, and already dreams for their marriage were being stripped away.

In the window seat, he swayed with the rattling train car. A dull glaze coated his eyes as he stared through the pane. She yearned to console him, to tell him he wasn't to blame. The Japanese pilots who'd decimated Pearl Harbor, a place she had heard of only that morning, had nothing to do with him.

You're an American, she wanted to say, *as American as I am, and we'll get through this together.*

But the sentence wound like a ball of wire in her throat, tense as the air around them. Any utterance would carry the projection of a scream in the muted coach. Helpless for an alternative, she inched her hand over to reunite with his. She made a conscious effort to evade scrutinizers' eyes. Closure around Lane's fingers jarred him from his reverie and he turned to face her. A warm half-smile rewarded her gesture. Then he glanced up as though recalling their audience, and the corners of his mouth fell. He squeezed her palm once, a message in the release, before leaning away.

For the rest of the trip, this was how they remained. Divided by a wall they'd had no say in constructing. Through the night hours, she heard him toss and turn on the berth beneath her; through the daylight hours, his gaze latched onto the mountains and valleys hurtling past.

Upon their debarking in Los Angeles, the contrast between Friday and Monday struck her like a slap.

It seemed mere moments ago when she had stood on this platform, the same suitcase at her feet. Yet everything had since changed.

'Extra, extra!' the paperboy in the station hollered. 'U.S. going to war! Read all about it!' His pitch carried easily over the graveness of the crowd. In small huddles, customers followed his order with newspapers propped in their hands. Headlines blared in thick black letters.

'Do you want me to come home with you?' Maddie asked Lane as they exited the station. The rustiness of her voice underscored the length of their silence.

'Nah, you'd best get home.'

'Are you sure?'

'Your brother's got to be worried about you. It's better if I check on my family alone.'

Of course. Nobody back here knew about their secret excursion. Now was hardly the time to announce their blissful news.

Lane added, 'I'll have a cab drop you on the way to my house, all right?'

She agreed, relieved they'd be together a little longer before facing the unknown.

A peaceful sunset glowed orange and pink as they approached the taxi stop. Lane swung open the back door of a Checker cab, inviting Maddie to slide in. He ducked in after her to take his seat.

'Whoa there, buddy!' the driver called out. 'Uh-uh, no way. I ain't driving no Jap.'

Lane became a statue, one leg in, one out.

'You heard me, pal!' The cabbie white-knuckled his steering wheel. Bystanders paused to observe the scene, pointing, not bothering to whisper.

'It's okay,' Maddie assured the driver, 'we're getting out.' She scooted back toward Lane, who blocked her from rising.

'No,' he told her. 'You go ahead.'

'But, Lane . . .'

'I'll take the next one.'

'Well – what if they won't—'

'Then I'll ride the bus.'

The driver's steely look bounced off the rearview mirror. 'You goin' or not, lady? Make up your mind.'

Lane tenderly touched her chin. 'Honey, don't worry. I'll swing by as soon as I can.' The surety in his tone caused her to relent. She made room for him to place her suitcase beside her. He had barely closed the door when the cabbie screeched away with the speed and power of fear.

Maddie strained to keep Lane in her view until the taxi veered around a corner. Grip on her luggage, she sat back in her seat.

Seven days, she told herself as they rumbled down streets that now felt foreign. In seven days God had created the Earth. In a single day mankind had turned it upside down.

CHAPTER 14

Free hand curled into a fist, TJ waited for the call to connect. Any more pacing and his shoes would leave a permanent groove in the floor. His ear felt feverish against the metal receiver. Behind him in the living room, a floor model radio delivered seeds of hysteria. The quiet of dusk amplified the man's reports: mandated blackouts, potential sub sightings, a climbing toll of Navy casualties, a list of precautions to keep families safe.

At last came a buzzing on the line. Years lingered between each ring.

'Answer it,' TJ snapped.

Another ring . . . and another . . .

'Allisters.' It was one of Jo's brothers, didn't matter which. They all sounded alike.

'It's TJ Kern. I was wondering—'

'*Who?*' The question competed with chaotic conversations in the background.

'TJ,' he repeated louder.

'You callin' about the meeting?'

'Meeting?' TJ said, thrown off.

'The block meeting.' The guy sounded annoyed.

'For standing guard at the beaches. We're figuring out shifts. You wanna come, we'll pick you up on the way.'

Jesus. Were enemies invading the coast? TJ had never even held a rifle before. Apparently it was time he learned.

'Uh, yeah. Okay.'

'Fine. See ya soon.'

Then TJ recalled his greater concern. 'Wait, don't hang up.'

A mumbled response trickled through, indiscernible amid the noise.

'I was looking for Maddie. I know she and Jo were supposed to be up north, visiting—'

'Hang on.' He yelled in a muffle, 'Shut your traps, will ya?' The volume lowered half a notch. 'Now, what're you sayin'?'

TJ rubbed his thumb over the knuckle of his fist, bridling his own annoyance. 'I was asking about Jo.'

'Hey, Jo! Phone's for you!' TJ winced from the guy hollering into the mouthpiece. A rustling and a clunk followed.

As TJ waited, relief swept over him. Jo was back in town. That meant Maddie must have stopped over at the Allisters' on the way home.

'Hello?'

'Jo. Thank God. Is Maddie still there?'

'TJ, is that you? Here, let me go in the other room.' More sounds of rustling with the handset and cord, then the chatter dimmed. 'I swear, I can't hear myself think in this place.'

No wonder she retreated to the ballpark to find some peace.

'I was just trying to find Maddie,' he said, 'since I hadn't heard from her yet.'

'Oh. I don't know. She didn't tell me what time she'd be home from her trip.'

'I – don't understand. Didn't you two travel together?'

'Together? No. Why's that?'

He wasn't in the mood for razzing, if that's what this was. 'To visit your cousins. In Sacramento.' The lengthy pause reinstated his panic. 'Jo, where the hell's my sister?'

He heard her exhale, at a loss. 'I don't know, TJ. . . . I don't know.'

'*I repeat,*' the broadcaster declared, '*we are in a state of emergency. Authorities recommend that everyone stay inside and tune in for further details.*'

A state of emergency. The death count rising.

In a combustive flash, he saw his father on the hospital bed. His mother lay lifeless on a silver table so shiny he could make out his own reflection. The memory of rain pelted his eardrums, interrupted by the screech of brakes.

But that screech was real. A fresh sound. He turned to the window.

'TJ? You there?' Jo said.

Maddie was stepping out of a taxi in a coat and hat, yet relief had no chance of regaining its footing. 'She's here,' he said, and slammed the handset onto the cradle. The bell inside pinged.

TJ faced the door with arms crossed. Air labored through his nose. He was a bull preparing to charge.

She didn't see him until she'd closed the door behind her and set down her case. Her demeanor shrank beneath his gaze.

'Where the *hell* have you been? And don't you dare lie to me again.'

Flushing, she fumbled for a reply.

'There's a goddamned war going on out there. You understand that? Got any idea what that means?'

She straightened, lifting her chin in feeble defiance. 'As a matter of fact, I do.'

'Yeah? Then why don't you prove it by telling me where you've *really* been.' He pressed her with a hard stare.

'I . . . think we should discuss this later. When you've had a chance to calm down.'

The challenge to his temper only inflamed it more. 'Well, that ain't gonna happen for a while. So why don't you start explaining yourself.'

She locked on his eyes and replied firmly. 'You're not my father, TJ.'

'You're right. But maybe I shoulda been. I guarantee, then, you wouldn't be traipsing all over the place with God-knows-who, doing—' An impossible sight cut through his words. A gold band gleamed from Maddie's finger. Her wedding finger.

She wouldn't . . . couldn't have. Yet the evidence was smack in front of him.

'You got married?' he breathed.

Her gaze fell to the ring. The answer was clear. What he didn't understand was why. Why'd she run off and elope? Why'd she keep it from him? His mind seized the most obvious reason, and the air in his lungs turned to lead.

'Maddie, are you pregnant?'

Her forehead bunched. 'Oh, God, no.' She gave an insistent shake of her head. 'No, it's nothing like that.' She reached for his arm, but he moved backward.

TJ wanted to feel grateful, but all he could think about was which asshole was responsible. Which one would trade a girl's innocence for lustful kicks. Why else would a guy have persuaded her to sneak around? Anyone with good intentions would have been up-front, not treated her like a dirty secret. Like a mistress. Like a whore.

He muscled down the thoughts. Left to roam free they just might unlock the cage inside, setting loose the constant rage that prowled back and forth behind the bars.

A succession of honks summoned his face toward the window. The silhouette of a pickup appeared, its headlights off.

'Come on, Kern! Let's move it!' Jo's brothers, plus a few other neighbors, crammed the truck from cab to bed. The fading sunset outlined their rifles pointed straight at heaven.

TJ grabbed his jacket from the coat tree. With

any luck, he could take his fury out on an enemy bomber orphaned from its flock.

'Where are you going?' Maddie asked as he headed for the door. 'TJ . . . ,' she pleaded.

In need of escape, he simply walked out.

CHAPTER 15

From the far corner of the lawn, Lane stared at the crime scene, his senses gone numb. No lights shone through the windows. By government order, darkness draped the city.

Men in black trench coats, black hats, even blacker eyes, swam in and out through the front door. They carried boxes off the small porch and down the driveway, loaded them into two old Packards with rear suicide doors.

FBI agents.

He recognized their type from the picture shows. That's what this had to be – a movie set. It wasn't real. At any moment, the word *Cut!* would boom from a director's horn and Cecil B. DeMille would leap from the trimmed hedges.

'Sir, you're gonna have to clear out.' The man approached him on the grass. His features were like Gary Cooper's, but spread over an elongated face.

When Lane didn't respond, the guy sighed, took another tack. 'I can see you're concerned about the family. But right now, they're part of an investigation. So I gotta ask you to move on till we're done. I know you people like your privacy, and I'm sure the Moritomos are no different.'

The mention of his surname – Moritomo, how did the fellow know that? – tore Lane from the surreal dimension of his hopes. There would be no intermission between reels, no velvet curtains or salted popcorn. Dramas crafted for the silver screen were morphing into the reality of his life.

'Listen, pal.' The agent planted a fist on his hip. 'I've asked you nicely, but if you're not gonna abide—'

'They're mine.' Lane's reply emerged with so little power he barely heard it himself. 'The family in there is mine.'

The man studied him and licked his bottom lip. He nodded toward the house. 'Well, then you'd better go in. Agent Walsh will have some questions for you.'

Lane scarcely registered the path he traveled that led him into the foyer. He was a driver after a weary day who had blinked and discovered he'd already reached his destination.

'*Onīsan!*' Emma came running. She latched onto his waist. Her little body trembled.

He set down his suitcase to rub the crown of her head. 'What's going on, Em? Where's Papa?'

She peeked over her shoulder and pointed toward the kitchen. Her manner indicated that the monster trapped in her closet had found a way out. Lane knelt on the slate and clasped his sister's hands.

It dawned on him how rapidly she had grown. He once could cover her entire fist with his palm. 'You go to your room while I figure out what's happening, okay?'

'But those men, they keep going in there.'

'Your bedroom?'

She nodded with a frown. 'They're looking through all my stuff. They took Papa's work books, and his radio, and his camera. Some of my Japanese tests too – even though I don't care about that.' Then, cupping her mouth, she whispered, 'I hid Sarah Mae so they couldn't find her.'

He was about to assure her that the doll he'd given her two Christmases ago wouldn't be in jeopardy. But who knew what they were looking for, or what other absurd belongings they would confiscate.

'Good thinking,' he told her. 'Now, you just sit on the stairs here. Everything's going to be all right.'

Reluctantly, she stepped back and sat on the middle step. She gripped the bars of the banister and watched him through a gap.

Lane paused while passing the parlor. Cushions of their empire couch had been slashed. Its stuffing poured out like foam. Scraps of papers dappled the rug. His father's prized katana swords had been pillaged from the wall.

A man's husky voice, presumably Agent Walsh's, led Lane into the kitchen. An oil lamp on the table soaked the room in yellow.

'You're not lying to me, are you, folks?' The guy, thick with a double chin and a round belly obscuring his belt, loomed over Lane's parents, who sat stiff and humble in their chairs. He held up a small laughing Buddha statue. ''Cause I don't want to wonder what else you might be hiding from me.'

'We telling the truth,' Lane's father insisted politely, taking obvious care to pronounce his words. 'We Christians. Not Buddhists. Christians. This only Hotei-*san*.'

'This is what?' Walsh said.

'Hotei,' Lane replied, turning them. 'It's a lucky charm. My mother brought it from Japan when they first moved here.'

'Uh-huh. And who might you be?'

'I'm their son.'

'Is that right,' Walsh said slowly, and glanced at Lane's father. 'I was told you were away at a university. How 'bout that, now?'

Lane fought to control his tone. If his dad possessed any trait, it was integrity. 'My train just got in. With a war starting, I thought I should be with my family.'

'Sure, sure. I understand,' the agent said, as though not accusing. He returned to Lane's mother in a gentle appeal. 'Got a family of my own. Nice, pretty wife, two kids. Boy and girl, just like yours. So I know how it is, wanting to do everything I can to protect them. Which is the reason we need to ask all these questions.' He put the decoration on the coffee table and motioned at Lane. 'Have a seat. Make yourself comfortable.' The arrogance of his invitation, implying a staked claim on the house, bristled the tiny hairs on Lane's neck.

Due to alien land laws, and Asian immigrants being barred from citizenship, his father could only lease the place. Although it was common practice, Lane hadn't felt right about purchasing it in his own name to bypass the rules. He preferred to change the system and guide society's evolution.

That system, however, was turning out more flawed than Lane thought – starting with Agent Walsh, who eyed him, waiting for compliance.

'I'm fine standing,' Lane bit out.

'Uh-huh. Well, I'm telling you to take a seat.'

'And I said I'm fine.'

Their invisible push and pull raised the temperature of the room.

'Takeshi, *suwarinasai*.' His father intervened, a stern command to sit.

Lane's gaze shot to his mother. The woman would never stand for such humiliation. After all, they had nothing to hide. But she remained rigid, her eyes fixed on the agent's dress shoes, another insult to their home. That's when Lane remembered he, too, hadn't taken his off.

'Boss,' a voice called out. The Gary Cooper agent entered the kitchen. 'I think we got something here.'

Walsh accepted a stack of large creased pages. Flickers from the lamp concealed the content from

Lane's view. The man flipped through them and drew out a whistle. 'So you like airplanes, do you, Mr Moritomo?'

'Yes, yes.' Lane's father perked with a touch of enthusiasm.

'American bombers . . . fighter planes . . . all kinds, looks like.'

'Yes, yes. I paint for, *ee* . . .' He searched for the word, found it. 'Hobby. Is hobby.'

'Any chance you've been sharing some of these drawings with, oh I don't know, friends back in Japan?'

Blueprints. That's what they'd found. Blueprints for his model aircrafts. The same ones any kid could buy for a few nickels at Woolworth's.

'This is ridiculous,' Lane blurted. 'Are you trying to say my father's a spy?'

Walsh crinkled the paper edges in his hands. 'Better watch that tone, son.'

'I'm not your son. And my father's not a criminal.' This wasn't how America worked. Justice, democracy, liberty – these were the country's foundational blocks that creeps like this kicked aside like pebbles.

Lane's father stood up and yelled, 'Takeshi! *Damarinasai.*'

'No,' Lane said, 'I won't be quiet. They can't come in here and do this. We haven't done anything. We're *not* the enemy.' Holding his gaze, he implored his father to fight for the very ideals with which Lane had been raised. Yet the man

126

said nothing. His Japanese roots had taken over, dictating his feudal servitude.

'Eh, Boss, we're all set.' A third guy appeared. The brim of his fedora shaded his features from nostrils up. 'Boss?'

Walsh relaxed his glower. 'Yeah?'

'All the major contraband's packed up.'

'Right.' He jerked his layered chin in Lane's direction. 'Then, let's take him in.' The two other agents crossed the room, the faceless one pulling out a pair of handcuffs.

Lane's stomach twisted. 'What is this? You're gonna arrest me?'

'Got a reason we shouldn't?' Walsh said.

Gary Cooper raised a calming hand at his supervisor. 'Al, you're tired. You need some food, some sleep. Go on home and rest up. We got this.'

Walsh exhaled, rubbed his eyes. Eventually, he mumbled his concession and handed off the blueprints. He had just left the kitchen when Lane heard two metallic ripples. The third agent had handcuffed his father, explaining it as a formality.

'*Nani ga atta no?*' Lane's mother demanded, now on her feet.

'We just need your husband for some more questioning,' the agent said. 'He'll be back by morning.'

'*Shinpai suruna,*' her husband assured her weakly as the men began escorting him out. '*Shikata ga nai.*'

Lane despised the old adage. *It can't be helped.* No culture needed to be so damn passive.

'You can't do this!' Lane marched behind them. 'Where are you taking him?'

'The Justice Department will be in touch,' one of them answered, right as Emma charged down the stairs, begging him to stay.

'Papa, *ikanaide.*' She shook his bound arms. 'Papa, Papa! *Ittara dame!*'

He offered her phrases of comfort that did little good. Then he turned to Lane and in Japanese stated in an even tone, 'From now on, you are responsible for the family.'

These were his final words before being ushered into the backseat of the agents' car, the last instructions before Emma chased them two full blocks. She wailed out useless pleas as her mother retreated into the dishevelment of their house. Neighbors peeked from windows.

Yet for Lane, none of this – not the groundless arrest, not his sister's cries nor their mother's isolation – caused the physical blow that came from the look in his father's eyes. A look of utter shame.

CHAPTER 16

She couldn't stand the wait anymore.

Maddie threw her coat back on, not bothering to fasten the buttons. She had tried phoning Lane, to confirm he'd made it home. Then to warn him not to come over. But the calls wouldn't go through. The only person she'd reached was Jo, who had more questions than Maddie felt up for. A third attempt to ring Lane's house had failed. The chaos of the switchboard was likely the problem, the operator had said. Told her to try again after a spell.

Maddie, though, didn't have time to spare. TJ could return at any minute – having gone to a meeting, Jo claimed. Right or wrong, TJ needed a chance to cool off before connecting her wedding band to Lane. And that's precisely what would happen if the three of them shared an exchange. After the intimacy of her wedding night, how could she possibly hide her feelings in Lane's presence?

In the morning, once TJ's shock had settled, she could explain everything. Rarely did she deviate from tracks laid in reason. He knew this. He knew *her.*

At least the brother she used to know did.

Headed for Lane's, she hurried from the house and down the front stairs. The tip of her shoe caught on the splintery bottom step, sending her tumbling. Exhaustion from the day wilted her body. No chance to rest. She heaved herself up and brushed off her gritty palms. A hole tore through her silk stockings, among the few she owned. Yet the misfortune had become a meaningless hiccup in the grand scheme.

She continued toward the street with a hindered stride. At this pace, the walk would stretch to a good twenty minutes, widening the opportunity for the guys to cross paths.

Should she go or stay? Which option would be worth the risk?

Frustrated by her own indecision, she wagered her hopes on a car approaching from the end of the long suburban street. The vehicle rumbled in and out of moonlight slanting between houses. Its chrome grille had the opened fish-mouth shape of a Buick's.

'Lane, please be you.' She focused on the windshield, breath held.

'Are you all right, dearie?' a woman called. It was her elderly neighbor, leaning out from behind her screen door. 'I was just watering my pansies in the window when I saw you take a fall.'

'Oh, yes, I'll be fine.' Maddie flung the reply behind her.

'I have some peroxide if you scraped yourself up.

You remember what I told you about my nephew's ankle, after he didn't care for it properly. Ended up almost dying in the hospital.'

No matter how dire the situation, Maddie knew better than to entrap herself in the house of a person who took pride in enumerating worst-case scenarios.

'I appreciate the offer. But I'll be okay.' Maddie stretched her neck toward the street.

'What are you doing out here, exactly? If you pardon my asking.'

'Just waiting for . . . a friend,' she said, at last determining that Lane – thank goodness – was the driver behind the wheel.

'Well,' the woman replied, 'if you change your mind.'

A creak indicated the screen door had shut, but Maddie could sense the peering of curious eyes.

Thoughts roaming in a fog, Lane pulled over slowly to the curb. He didn't notice Maddie waiting outside until she bolted around the hood to reach him. As he stepped out of the car, she spoke in a quiet rush.

'TJ's on a rampage. If he finds out about us tonight, I don't know what he'll do. I tried to call your house, to warn you not to come over, but I couldn't get through.'

Lane fixed his attention on her lips. Their movements shaped syllables that had become hard for him to grasp.

'Sweetheart,' she said. 'Did you hear me?'

'They cut our lines,' he heard himself say.

'They what?'

'Cut our phone lines. The FBI arrested my father. Took boxes full of our things.'

She covered the base of her neck with her hand. 'But – why?'

The image of his dad being driven away, handcuffed like a criminal, came charging back. The insanity of it all beat like a fist behind his forehead. 'They said they needed him for more questioning. They're wasting time. I'm telling you, he had nothing to do with it.'

'Of course he didn't,' Maddie said in natural agreement.

Lane raked his hand through his hair. Why did he feel the need to present her with his case?

'Oh, honey, you'll figure this out. You always do.' Her eyes shone with belief, a deepened trust that he could conquer any obstacle. But rather than it fortifying him, for the first time ever, he felt afraid of failing her.

'How is Emma?' she asked. 'And your mom?'

'They're all right. Or they will be, once my dad is back.' By morning. That's what the agent had said. If not, Lane would find a way to bring him home. He had to. 'I'll come by as soon as I know more.'

'Why don't I stop over instead? At your house sometime tomorrow?'

The house. Shredded to pieces.

'We'll see.'

In the awkward silence, she glanced at the neighboring home. Was she nervous about their being seen together? Lane had grown accustomed to keeping their relationship under wraps, but he'd presumed that would change after their vows.

'I've gotta go.' He started to duck into the car.

'Just a minute.' She clutched his hand on the rim of the door. 'I wanted to say that – no matter what – I hope you know that . . .' She trailed off, enwrapped him with her arms. Against his cheek, she finished in a heartfelt whisper, 'I love you, Lane. I love you so much.'

His eyelids lowered, blocking out all but the warmth of her breath, the softness of her hair and body. They were again in that hotel suite, curled up under the oblivion of the sheets. A complimentary bowl of nuts and fruit adorned the bureau. It could have sustained them for at least another day. Why, in God's name, did he ever let them leave that room?

Maddie yanked herself from his hold, and the illusion followed her.

'Tomo, you're here,' TJ called to him, rounding the corner. 'What's going on?'

This was Lane's cue for quick thinking – but nothing came. His excuses had run dry.

'Tomo?'

Maddie jumped in. 'Where did you go, TJ? Where are the others?'

He looked at Lane curiously. 'Just had a meeting.

They drove back to their place afterward. I walked from there.'

She snuck Lane a glance, a plea for him to act natural. 'So, the meeting. What was that about?'

TJ's attention traveled between him and Maddie in calculating progression. 'Shooting the enemy,' he replied, distracted. A struggle between denial and the obvious escalated in his eyes. His shoulders lifted an inch.

In light of all that was happening, Lane couldn't do this anymore. They needed to protect one another. And that couldn't happen until he fessed up.

'Lane was actually just leaving,' Maddie said. 'He has to see about his family. Isn't that right?'

A beat dragged past before Lane could push out the words. 'TJ, I think we need to talk.'

'Lane,' Maddie breathed. 'Please.'

TJ's gaze lowered, sharply halting at the ring on Lane's finger. His jaw visibly tightened. 'What have you done?'

Something plummeted and landed hard in Lane's chest. 'We should go inside.'

'No,' he said. 'You tell me now.'

Maddie's arms closed over her chest, her neck drawn. She appeared ready for an earthquake. Clearly she had forgotten, as had Lane until this moment, that he and TJ were blood brothers. Two pricks of a sewing needle had sealed their bond in the storage room of Mr Kern's shop. They were eight, but their pact held no expiration. Nothing could divide them.

Not even this.

Lane closed the car door. He faced TJ before speaking. 'Months ago, Maddie and I, we started dating. We were afraid how you might feel about that, really about her dating anyone. So, we thought it'd be better not to say anything – just at first, though.'

TJ broke in with a slow, raw voice: 'Did. You. Marry her?'

No amount of padding would cushion the truth. Lane took a weary breath and answered. 'Yes.'

Disappointment carved its way into TJ's face. It was then that Lane imagined how it would feel, down the road, if some guy ran off and married Emma. Let alone his best pal.

Maddie attempted a voice of reason, which TJ shut down by trudging toward the house.

'Hold on.' Lane followed him. 'I know it looks terrible. And I'm sorry, honest I am. But you have to let me explain.'

The air turned electric as TJ reached the stairs. A single spark could set off an explosion. Still, Lane couldn't let him think the worst.

'Buddy, listen to me,' he said, catching TJ's elbow.

In an instant, TJ swung around and grabbed him by the shirt, cinched it up under Lane's chin. 'I'm not listening to anything from you! I ought to kill you, you piece of shit!'

'*Stop it,*' Maddie shrieked. She worked to restrain her brother, his right arm poised for a punch.

'Go on,' Lane yelled back. 'Hit me.' And he meant it, wanted the redemption found in a rightful punishment. 'Do it!'

'That's enough,' Maddie said.

TJ's fist quavered, as did his reddened face. Releasing his grip, he shoved Lane back several feet. 'You were supposed to be my friend.'

Lane's hand rose to his gathered collar. 'I *am* your friend.'

'No, you're not. You're a filthy liar,' he seethed. 'Paul was right. You're just another dirty yellow Jap.'

Maddie protectively held Lane's arm. 'TJ, you don't mean that.'

Whether he did or not, the result was the same. The floor in Lane's gut had dropped out, leaving him hollowed. A shell unable to move.

'Get back in the house,' he told his sister.

'*No.*'

'I told you to get back inside!'

'Or what? You're going to hit me too?'

Something pulled TJ's head up. Lane followed his gaze to find neighbors in their entries, watching the show. When he returned his focus to TJ, the emotion in the guy's eyes launched a chill over Lane's skin. Disappointment had dissolved into hatred.

'Get the hell off our property. I don't ever want to see you again.' With that, TJ went into the house.

Maddie stared after her brother as their audience ebbed away. 'I should've told him from the beginning. This is all my fault.'

'No,' Lane contended. 'I'm just as much to blame.' Tough as it was to face, he could have confessed at any time. Yet he hadn't. Not just because Maddie had asked him to wait, but because he'd been willing to sacrifice anything to ensure they stayed together.

Drained of words, they moved to the driver's side of the car. As he squeezed the door handle, Maddie clasped his hand. 'Let me come stay with you.'

On any other day, he would have rejoiced over living with her. But for now, aside from a guaranteed objection from his mother – undoubtedly heightened by the situation – the FBI could return without notice, interrogating anyone with links to his family. The last thing he'd do was subject Maddie to that treatment.

'Believe me, I wish you could.'

'I just need to grab my things,' she said. 'My luggage is still packed.'

'Not yet, sweetheart.'

'When, then?'

'I . . . don't know. When I head back to school, I suppose.'

School. Finals. Would they continue as scheduled, or be put on hold with the rest of his life?

'I don't want to be without you,' she said, her bottom lip trembling.

He shook his head and offered in assurance, 'You won't have to.' He brought her into his arms. 'This is only for now. Till things settle, it's safer for you here. Understand?'

She said nothing, but gave a reluctant nod.

'I'll call the shop and come see you when I can.' He kissed her on the forehead, then the lips. Her face conveyed a craving, a need for security he couldn't deny. 'Don't you worry,' he told her. 'Everything will work out.'

When she nodded again, he got into the car and drove away, half regretting what he'd said. For what was intended as a promise felt like yet another lie.

PART II

月に叢雲 花に嵐

Meaning of Japanese proverb:
Like clouds over the moon and storm over blossoms, misfortune often strikes during times of happiness.

CHAPTER 17

Two days and still no word from him. Maddie had arrived at the shop early that morning in search of a second letter from Lane. He had hand-delivered the first one through the mail slot on the door. Wrinkles from frequent readings covered the pages already imprinted in her memory.

My dearest Maddie,

I imagine this isn't the honeymoon you were hoping for. It certainly isn't the one I'd had in mind. At least when it comes to my arranged marriage, I won't have to find a way of letting the woman down gently. I think it's safe to assume the matchmaker has taken me out of the running. (That's supposed to make you laugh.)

On a more serious note, despite my efforts I haven't been able to locate my father. The sole explanation I've received is that they're holding him because of his position at the bank. Since the Sumitomo headquarters are in Tokyo and funds are constantly transferred back and forth, the Justice Department is investigating him thoroughly. Of course, he's not the only one. Japanese leaders and teachers are also being held. Even Christian ministers, if you can believe it.

That's what I've pieced together, anyhow, from what little the authorities will share. I've left several messages for Congressman Egan in hopes that he can speed up my father's release. I guess my dad's long-overdue bank promotion turned out to be a curse.

As for the rest, the last few days have been a blur. Between maintaining things at home and helping our Japanese neighbors turn in 'contraband' (as if eighty-year-old Mrs Kubota was going to use her RCA radio to coordinate a massive assault), I've barely had time to sit. Since the banks froze all Japanese accounts, we had to let our housekeeper go. On the upside, it's forced me and my sister to take up cooking. Most of the meals have even been edible. A husband who's handy in the kitchen. Who would've guessed?

Once things ease up, as I know they're bound to, we'll have a working phone again and I can call to hear your voice. Better still, you and I will have time to ourselves in person. In case I don't see you when I deliver this, please know I carry you always in my heart.

All my love,
Lane

Although he had brightened the letter with his usual touch of humor, Maddie could surmise the toll such hardships had to be taking on his family. To top it off, curfews were now imposed on the Japanese community, further reducing her opportunities to see Lane. Forces seemed intent on keeping them apart. Her brother most of all.

TJ had actually demanded she file for divorce, or an annulment if possible, to reverse her 'mistake.' A mistake! Like she'd simply mistuned her violin or forgotten an appointment.

She stamped out the thought as she worked.

At her sewing machine, she guided the pumping needle over the dress draped across her lap. The tangerine fabric, with its grid of yellow lines, could cause a traffic jam from the glare. Not to mention the maddening chore of shrinking the garb by five full sizes.

'Sugar,' Bea drawled, returning from the back room, 'would you watch the store for a bit?' She set a package wrapped in tan paper on the reception counter and retrieved her purse from a drawer.

'I'd be happy to,' Maddie said, though Bea's errand seemed curious. Drop-offs for regular customers happened on occasion, but typically after closing hours, not in the middle of the day. 'Are you making a special delivery?' she asked.

'It's for Mrs Duchovny.'

Ah, yes . . . her son's shirt. The one with blue pinstripes that needed a button replaced. His mother had brought it here the day Lane had proposed at the beach. And to think, Maddie had gone there with the notion they were going to break up.

As Bea shrugged into her pink knit sweater, Maddie said, 'If you'd like, I could drop those off on my way home. Save you the trip.' The Duchovnys lived only a couple blocks from Maddie's house. Besides, the complimentary service seemed the least she could do to show gratitude for her benefactress. 'Or, I could go now if they need the clothes earlier.'

Bea ran her fingers across the package, her coral lips pursed. Sunlight through the window reflected off the sides of her silvery bun. 'I suppose there's no real rush. Since hearing the news, I just feel awful that some of his belongings aren't where they ought to be.' The sullenness in her tone struck Maddie's ears like an off-key chord.

'What do you mean? What news?'

'Oh, sugar. I thought – well, I assumed you'd heard, what with your ties to the family and all.'

Maddie clenched her wedding band, which hung on a necklace beneath her blouse. There it raised fewer questions, while providing strength when needed.

'I'm afraid it's not good, dear,' Bea explained. 'I'm so sorry to be the one to tell you, but . . . when the *Arizona* sank' – she paused – 'Donnie was on it.'

A sharp exhale slipped out before Maddie could

cover her mouth. Donnie Duchovny. He'd been a classmate of hers since grade school. A nice boy – one who blended. He used to weave his pencil over his knuckles during tests. She had forgotten that. Forgotten about his naval station. How was that possible, after listening to his mother's boasting since the day he'd enlisted, no subtler than her matchmaking hints for Maddie?

'That poor family,' Bea sighed. 'Bless her heart, Mrs Duchovny was so excited about their boy coming home for Christmas too. And those book-shelves his daddy made for him . . .' Bea angled her face away to discreetly dab the corners of her eyes. It was the first time Maddie had seen her shed a tear. 'Gracious, would you look at me. I'd better pull myself together. They certainly don't need me adding to their woes.'

'I'll take it.'

At Bea's startle, Maddie considered what she had just volunteered. It wasn't too late to retract the offer. Nonetheless, delivering the parcel herself would be the right thing to do. Not only had the Duchovnys promised financial help with Juilliard, soon after her father moved into the rest home, but Donnie's shirt had remained at the shop because of Maddie.

'Oh, sugar,' Bea said, 'I didn't mean to imply you needed to take on the job.'

'You did nothing of the sort. I'd just like to do it, if you wouldn't mind.'

Bea gave this some thought. Then she passed the wrapped garments over with reverent care.

Maddie nodded and headed for the streetcar. Only upon settling into her seat did she register the incongruent weight of the package. It felt much too light to be carrying the memory of a person's soul.

Two sets of light knocks on the door failed to summon an answer. Maddie couldn't bring herself to pound. Although tempted to leave the bundle beside the planter box, as she'd done in the past, she knew the situation called for a personal delivery. No question, her father would have demanded it, even done this himself if still capable. She could imagine him verbalizing as much, clear as the concertos stored in her head.

While visiting him yesterday, updating him on all that had happened with Lane and TJ, she'd received the usual static response. On her way out, though, she swore she'd heard a whisper, an urging that she and her brother make up, that they tear down their barricade of silence.

It was merely her conscience speaking.

Maddie resorted to pressing the doorbell, and heard the ring inside. Not the frazzled buzz of her own house, but an elegant *ding-dong* to match the two-story, powder-blue Victorian home. Aside from the faint rattling of a car, the area had become devoid of sound. As though the death of a resident had triggered a mute switch in the neighborhood.

She tried the bell once more. Still no answer. A service flag hung in the window. Donnie's single blue star would soon be gold, a symbol of his sacrifice. Boys scarcely of age were enlisting in droves. Estimates claimed the war would be over in months. But how many gold stars would accumulate before then?

Troubled by the notion, at the recollection of mourning, Maddie decided to come back later. She pivoted to leave – just as the door yawned open. There stood a portly woman in a bathrobe. The scarf enveloping her hair was knotted at the top behind a frizzy lock. No rouge on her cheeks, no color on her lips. Puffy bags lined her eyes.

Maddie almost didn't recognize the customer she'd known since childhood.

'What do you want?' she ground out.

'I'm sorry to bother you.' Maddie grappled for words. 'It was rude of me not to call first.'

Mrs Duchovny watched her dully. A painful quiet passed back and forth.

Maddie lifted the parcel. 'I thought – that is, Beatrice suggested you might want these.' Mrs Duchovny didn't extend her hands, prompting Maddie to clarify. 'Your jacket is done. The lovely green one.' She took a breath. 'And the shirt.'

The woman made no reply at first. Then a soft, 'Donnie's.'

Maddie raised the package higher as a means of affirmation.

Hesitant at first, Mrs Duchovny took the bundle and hugged it to her middle. The paper crackled from the pressure.

Maddie staved off her emotions by rushing through their parting. 'I'm terribly sorry for your loss. Please let me know if there's anything we can do.' Not expecting a response, she dipped her head and started for the rock path that edged the manicured lawn.

'Is it true?'

The question rooted Maddie's shoes. Over her shoulder, she asked, 'Pardon?'

'I said, *Is it true?*' More than irritation powered the huskiness of her tone. Alarm, perhaps. Desperation.

Maddie stepped closer, racking her brain for context. Was Mrs Duchovny asking if her son was actually dead, versus purely a rumor?

Newspapers had detailed the attack in which nearly three thousand perished. There would be no body for confirmation, Maddie realized, if Donnie had drowned while trapped in the ship. The same went for those burned beyond recognition.

How ever was she to answer?

'Mrs Duchovny . . . ,' she began.

'I want to know. Is it true what your neighbors are saying?' The woman's intensity rose. 'Tell me you didn't marry a Jap. Tell me you didn't devote yourself, before the eyes of God, to a man whose people murdered my only child.'

Just like that, the air turned to glass; shards scraped Maddie's throat with every breath. A reply had no chance of passing through, leaving silence to confirm the truth.

And for this, Mrs Duchovny's face, usually warm and doughy, petrified with disgust. Her eyes glinted like steel, cool as the hidden ring dangling from Maddie's neck.

'Madeline Kern. You ought to be thankful your parents aren't here to see this day. The shame would be unbearable.'

When the door slammed, Maddie winced, letting loose a tear. It blazed down her cheek and vanished on the worsted mat.

CHAPTER 18

TJ lost all awareness of his surroundings until someone gripped his arm. He spun around.

'Easy there, slugger.' Jo laughed with a start.

He relaxed his fist, dropped it to his side. 'Hey, Jo.'

'You know, for a second there, I was thinking you were ignoring me,' she teased. 'I was in the window and you walked right by. I must've hollered your name half a dozen times.'

TJ glanced past her. A block down, white letters appeared on the glass pane. *Allister's Hardware.* He'd ridden the bus home from campus entrenched in thought, and evidently gotten off two stops early.

'Been studying hard?' She motioned to the canvas satchel on his shoulder.

With Maddie's situation playing havoc with his concentration, the afternoon he'd just spent at the library had been a waste. 'Finals are next week, so I gotta buckle down. See you around, though, all right?'

He was about to walk away when she said, 'I just clocked out for the day, and I'm dying for a Coke. You thirsty?'

Definitely sounded better than hitting the books. But, he reminded himself, a scholarship hung in the balance. 'Believe me, wish I could.'

As two Navy men strolled past them, he half expected Jo's eyes to follow – all the girls seemed to have gone ape over the uniforms – but her attention didn't stray. It was only her expression that changed. More serious now.

'You can talk to me, if you want. 'Bout what happened with Lane.' Her eyes penetrated him with a look of understanding, same as from the night on the baseball mound.

'Maddie told you.'

She shrugged.

'Dandy,' he muttered.

'So, how about it?' Jo produced a small wad of greenbacks from a pocket of her work uniform. 'First one's on me.'

Tempted by her company, he checked his watch. His sister would be returning from work soon. Their mutual silence aside, he was still obligated to keep an eye on her.

Jo jabbed him playfully in the ribs. 'Come on, it's fuel for the brain. A tall glass of Coke, *fizz-fizz-fizz*. Cherry syrup stirred in. Crispy fries, maybe? Mm-mm.'

Given that Maddie made a point of cooking only for one these days, a basket of fries did sound appetizing. 'Fine, you got me. But I can't stay long.'

'Deal.'

'And just so we're clear, I'm picking up the bill.' He couldn't let a girl pay.

'For a second, I was worried you weren't gonna offer.'

He laughed in spite of himself.

'Ooh, just remembered. I gotta tell Gramps about a toolbox on special order. Don't move a muscle.' She jogged off to the store, bound hair swinging, her energy infectious.

TJ shook his head. Who'd have predicted that Jo Allister, his kid sister's friend all these years, would turn out to be a pal of his too? It was nice, finding a gal who was so easy to chat with. Surprisingly, they had a good deal in common, from their family losses to sports to . . .

The thought stirred a memory from weeks ago – Jo yakking him up right before Lane showed at the house, the night they all went to the jazz club. He'd viewed her rambling about the World Series as an attempt to improve his mood. The real reason didn't become clear until now: Lane had come over to see Maddie, not him. Jo had known, and she'd let him play the idiot.

'Sorry about that,' Jo said, returning. 'You ready?'

TJ didn't move. 'Did you know about Lane and Maddie? That they'd planned to get hitched?'

Jo flinched, a double take. 'Well – no. I had no idea they were gonna run off and do that.'

'You knew they were dating, though.'

'Yeah,' she admitted, 'I knew, but . . . Maddie

promised she was going to tell you. And I think she really was, except then—'

'Save it.' He pierced her with a glare before striding away.

'TJ. Wait.'

He continued down the sidewalk and across the street, not acknowledging a car that hit the brakes for his passage. The driver honked.

'Would you have reacted any different,' Jo called out, 'if you'd known earlier?'

Oh yeah he would have. He would have stopped it from ever happening in the first place.

He just wished he could convince Maddie it wasn't too late to salvage her future. The arguments he'd presented had gotten them nowhere. She'd refuted them all until there was nothing left to say.

Maybe he'd been appealing to the wrong person. If he alone couldn't open her eyes, he could think of the one person who could.

CHAPTER 19

As Lane entered his house, the smell of smoke greeted him like an intruder. His internal alarm blasted in his ears, along with his father's words.

From now on, you are responsible for the family.

'Emma,' he yelled, charging toward the kitchen. '*Okāsan!*' Visions arose of a greased pan on fire, its orange and yellow flames climbing the walls. But once he got there, he discovered the kitchen in its normal state. Dishes were drying on the rack from breakfast. The Frigidaire buzzed long and low.

Smoke, not suggestive of food, continued to pave an invisible trail. And the faintest hint of gasoline. Was someone trying to run them out, a person who hated them enough to burn down their house – with or without his family inside?

'Emma!' he shouted, panic rising. He'd witnessed the crime in his dreams.

'I'm right here.' Emma's voice whipped him around.

'Where's the smoke coming from?'

In a rust-red jumper, she toted a box half her size, a trove of personal keepsakes. Sadness rimmed her eyes. 'It's *Okāsan*. She's in back, burning all the Japanese papers and other stuff we still had left.'

Lane mentally chided himself for assuming the worst. He'd forgotten that many other 'Issei' were doing the same. The immigrants had been destroying their letters and diaries, no matter how mundane; photographs of their youth spent in Japan, of their babies dressed in kimonos. A history erased as a show of loyalty.

'Do I really have to give her my school pictures?' Emma asked tightly. 'Can't I at least save the notes from my friends?'

He patted her braids, uneven and puckering from weaving them herself. 'You're not giving up a thing. Go put these back in your room, and let me talk to Mother.'

'But . . . she said I had to.'

'She won't mind, I promise. You go up and play now. Throw a tea party with Sarah Mae.'

Emma glanced at her rescued box, and a sparkle returned to her Betty Boop eyes. 'Will you come too?'

'You get everything ready, and I'll join you soon.'

When she shuffled toward the stairs, Lane headed for the door off the laundry room to stop his mother from this foolishness. Through the screen door he could see her. On the concrete patio, she sat primly on a wrought-iron chair. Black plumes swayed from a metal pail at her slippered feet. She lifted an envelope from the shoebox resting on her lap. Yet instead of adding it to the smoldering pile, she held the post to her chest and squeezed her eyes shut. The emotion crumpling her face glued Lane's grip to the door handle. He leaned back onto his heels, causing the screen door to squeak.

Her eyelids flew open. Again, she was a statue. *'Otōsan no kotode nanika kīta?'* Her tone remained flat, even while inquiring about news of her husband's arrest.

In response, Lane followed a longtime urge to enforce a change. 'We shouldn't speak Japanese anymore. We're Americans. We should act like it.'

'Demo, watakushi no eigo—'

'Your English is fine. I've heard you use it at stores when you have to.'

Her fingers tightened on the shoebox. Her deceptively dainty jaw lifted. *'Wakatta wa.'* She agreed in her native language, no doubt to make a point. Then she snatched a photo from the box and flung it into the pail.

Lane reached out, unable to save the memento in time. 'Mother, you don't have to do that.'

She watched the flames devour the corners with greedy bites. It was her wedding portrait, a picture he hadn't seen since boyhood. Heat animated their kimonos by bubbling the black-and-white image. Their stately pose gained a semblance of celebration it had never appeared to have. But then her headdress recoiled. Oval holes grew as if spurred by drops of acid, wiping away the bride's youth.

On occasion, Lane would recall a trace of the

innocence she'd once had. How she used to smile with a warmth that reached her eyes – like on the Mother's Day he had proudly given her a lopsided clay pot; or the morning his father had first launched a toy glider, after a month of painstaking assembly, only to have the plane crushed by a passing truck. His wife had burst into such unbridled giggles, she'd forgotten the cultural female habit of covering her mouth.

What had happened over the years to both thaw and return her to ice?

The sound of his name sliced through his pondering. His mother's impatience indicated she was repeating herself. She pointed to their house, where a doorbell rang. He could sense her desire for protection, despite an exhibition of strength.

'I'll get it.' Probably another junk dealer. Lane had shooed off two of the vultures this week. In cheap suits and tonic-saturated hair, they'd had the audacity to come here, citing reports of an impending Japanese American evacuation, offering to buy up belongings for half their worth. *Those* were the types of people who should be locked up by authorities.

He divulged none of this as he turned to go inside. While entering he glanced back, and a sight brought him pause. Something peeked out from his mother's sweater pocket. An envelope. The same one, he would guess, that he had caught her embracing. A family letter? He found it improbable, and not just because she was an only child.

Like most Issei, his parents' connections to kin in Japan essentially ended the minute they boarded the boat for a new life. Only in rare instances would he catch a relative's name tossed out, like a puff at a dandelion. Then, bound to its seeds, Lane's interest would just as soon drift away.

A double ring of the bell reminded him of the caller. He hastened toward the foyer and swung open the door. For a moment, he just stared.

On his porch was TJ Kern.

From beneath the curved lid of a baseball cap, TJ spoke first. 'Hey,' he said.

'Hi.'

A grueling quiet. 'So, I heard about your dad.'

The intent unclear, Lane found himself on the defense. 'They're just questioning him as a formality, because he worked at the bank.'

TJ shifted his weight, his hands jammed into the front pockets of his jeans. He nodded slowly, as if organizing his words. 'Listen, there were a lot of things said between us. But what's done is done. All that's important is how we move forward.'

Lane became aware, right then, how much he had been hoping for this conversation. Admittedly, TJ's words had left a bruise that continued to throb. But the fact was, the guy had made an effort by coming here.

Lane stepped out onto the porch. Beneath their shoes were the same planks they had sanded and repainted as kids, when their carved designs from TJ's new pocketknife weren't a hit with Lane's mom. They'd screwed up; they'd learned. They'd repaired the damage.

'I want you to know,' Lane said, 'that I *am* sorry. I shouldn't have kept it all from you, but you have to understand why.'

'Maddie told me.'

Lane blinked at this. Last he'd heard, she and her brother weren't on speaking terms. 'She explained – about the arranged marriage?'

'She told me enough,' he said. 'Besides, none of that matters. All I care about is how to square away this mess.'

Relaxing, Lane nodded. 'Believe me, I'd love to get back the way things were between you and me—'

'Lane, I'm not talking about you and me.' More jarring than the frustration in TJ's reply was the use of 'Lane' rather than 'Tomo.'

'Then what *are* we talking about?'

'Maybe you two did have a chance at making it. Maybe you actually thought through your finances, and job, and her schooling. Even where you were gonna live. But you've gotta see that the situation's changed.'

'It doesn't change how I feel about her.'

'I didn't say it did.'

'So what are you suggesting? That I walk away because things are tough right now?' Lane cringed at the idea of living without her. Seeing Maddie only twice over the past week had been hard enough. 'They're not going to stay this way. It'll all settle down.'

'Are you kidding?'

'Just hear me out—'

'We're in a goddamned war! With Japan, for Christ's sake. It's not fair what you're doing to her and you know it!'

Fair? The concept had become laughable. Lane's volume rose to the challenge. 'My family's being treated like criminals, and for what? Huh? What's fair about that?'

Their eyes held, a silent standoff.

How did they come to this?

What's more, how could Lane possibly do what TJ was asking?

Since the car accident, he understood TJ's protectiveness. But he also understood that Maddie had grown up without her brother noticing. Now Lane wanted to be the one to protect her, as a husband who cared for her as much as TJ. Maybe more.

'I love Maddie,' Lane told him. 'You have to know, I love her more than anything.'

Without pause, not even a humoring of consideration, TJ's answer came low and firm. 'Prove it, then. If you really love her, do what's best for her – by letting her go.'

The words sank in layer after layer. They reached down to the bruise inside, reviving a throb as TJ turned to leave.

When Lane finally went for the door, he found his mother in the entry. Darkness raged in her eyes. Lane waited for a rebuke, but none came. She simply gathered her anger and walked away.

CHAPTER 20

Impossible hand positions on stubborn strings nearly drove Maddie to fling her bow out her bedroom window. Through sixty-four phrases of a repetitive bass line, the notes marched in twos, then threes and fours. They waded through each maddening section of Bach's Chaconne, a fifteen-minute marathon of advanced arpeggios and chord progressions.

It had been two long months since America declared war. Yet her armor of melodies, until today, had managed to keep her emotions in check. Behind their shields, she could temporarily forget the empty visits with her father, even the resentment between her and TJ, masked by what had progressed to civil exchanges.

Perhaps Bach's partita itself was the problem. This movement had, after all, been their wedding processional. Now each measure of its three-beat bars reminded her of the perfect future she'd glimpsed with Lane, only to have it swiped clean from her fingers. Stolen by strangers.

But what else should she spend her time playing? Without the Duchovnys as benefactors, Juilliard was no longer an option. Thus, maintaining mastery of Mazas's Thirty-Sixth Opus or Viotti's Twenty-Second Concerto was pointless when auditioning would merely taunt her with what she couldn't have.

And so, she persisted in tackling the Chaconne, until her back ached and fingers whined. She obsessed over stumbled trills and missed double-stops. As if conquering the piece could close the gap forming between her and Lane. She could feel the void gaining mass every time they met. It stalked them at Hollenbeck Park, straining their conversations. It hovered in Lane's car as their bodies joined in the backseat, failed attempts to re-create the intimacy they'd once found.

She wanted to scream, to yell until the world came to its senses.

Instead, she trained her vision on the sheet music propped on the metal stand. Or at least she tried. An image in the lid of her violin case competed for her focus: a small copy of her wedding photo, taken by the minister's wife. There it was, nestled in a spot previously reserved for Mozart.

Common sense told her to shut the lid, but she couldn't. She needed to keep those memories alive. She reached out and traced Lane's smile, her mother's bouquet. Relationships, like spiderwebs, required such care in the beauty of their weaving – only to be severed by a single rain. There had to be something Maddie could do to prevent her marriage from meeting the same fate.

She glanced around the room, at belongings now bearing little value – the perfume bottles and figurines, the posters of classical performances. From the thought, a solution materialized. While no umbrella existed large enough to protect them, somewhere out there the skies shone clear.

On the Moritomos' front porch, Maddie crossed her arms, unwilling to yield. 'Give me one reason why.'

'I can give you a dozen,' Lane argued.

'I'm not talking about leaving forever. Just a month or two. Until things calm down, like you said.'

'Forget about what I said. Haven't you read the papers?'

She hadn't because she didn't have to. She'd overheard enough from customers in the shop – of suspected spies and espionage labeled 'Fifth Column' activity. From the Hearst and McClatchy newsies to coastal farmers and fishermen, anyone harboring anti-Oriental sentiments had been handed a long-awaited excuse to vent in the open.

If nothing else, her family's misfortune had taught her to recognize inflated dramatics for what they were. Gossip that would gradually lose its luster. Which was why her plan made sense.

'All of this is going to pass,' she persisted. 'Things will get better.'

'Or,' he said, 'they'll get even worse.' He spoke with a resignation that scared her.

'Lane, that can't be the case *everywhere*.'

'So you just want to pack up and run off?'

'We did it before, didn't we?'

'That was different.'

'How?' she challenged.

'Because I have my family to think about now.'

Maddie hadn't fully considered what it would be like to travel with his mother, a woman whose brittle silence spelled out displeasure over their marriage like the bold letters of a marquee.

'And what about your brother?' Lane added. 'Don't you think he's going to have something to say?'

'It isn't his decision. This is about you and me.'

'But it's not, Maddie. Not anymore.' He rubbed his temple as if fending off a headache.

Something else was troubling him. His father, maybe. They still hadn't heard from the man. Since his transfer to New Mexico – a detention center in Santa Fe – Lane had penned inquiries to more than a dozen officials, including the President.

'Have you received a reply,' she ventured carefully, 'from any of the letters you sent about your dad?'

'Nobody's answered,' he said. 'Well – except for one.'

'Oh? Who was it from?'

'Congressman Egan's office.'

The gentleman knew Lane personally. Of course he would be helpful.

'What did he say?'

'His secretary sent a letter. Said I should take up my concerns with the Department of Justice directly. And oh, by the way, with restructuring due to the war, they won't be in need of my services, after all.'

Maddie remembered the elation in Lane's voice the day they had offered him the job. She longed to hear that voice again.

He crossed the porch, gripped the rail with both hands, and stared into the muddled afternoon sky. She could see the light inside him dimming. Striving to keep it aglow, she followed him over and laid her hand on his back. He was wearing the maroon sweater-vest she had made him for Christmas. The annual holiday had grown grimmer – as would all the days if they stayed.

'I can imagine how horrible you must feel. But if you think about it, this is one more thing not keeping you here.'

'And what about your dad?' he said without looking at her.

'My dad?'

'Your visits. Don't you need to be there, to play for him every week?'

She almost replied that her father wouldn't notice. But then she saw a vision of him waiting by his window, even vaguely aware that his daughter had abandoned him, and her stomach turned cold.

'Besides,' Lane said, 'what would we live on? My parents' cash savings won't last forever, and who knows if we'll ever see our money from the bank. Then there's school to think about.' He shook his head and faced her. 'Just because I'm not going back doesn't mean you shouldn't follow your plans for New York.'

Although the timing wasn't ideal, she had to tell him. She'd been keeping it from him too long. 'I'm not going,' she interjected.

He looked at her as though she'd lost her marbles.

'With the war, it doesn't seem right,' she said. 'One more year isn't going to make a difference.'

'That's ridiculous. You have someone willing to pay your way. You can't turn that down.'

She wanted to avoid explaining. She'd lie if she could, yet his eyes forced out the truth. 'The Duchovnys have changed their minds. But it's all right. With all that's happening—'

'Why would they do that?'

The question conveyed more disbelief than bewilderment. Despite the challenge, she replied quietly, hoping to soften the impact. 'Their son. He died at Pearl Harbor.'

Layers of comprehension unfolded over Lane's face, followed by something more. His unjust, indirect responsibility in the matter. The revelation deepened the lines in his forehead he had only recently gained. 'How much is tuition?'

Maddie suspected where this was leading. 'It doesn't matter.'

'Just tell me.'

'It's too much, for either of us right now.'

'What's the amount?' he insisted.

'Fine. It's three hundred, but that's just for classes. Room and board is at least four hundred more, another two hundred for lunches and incidentals. So you see? It's an outrageous amount for anyone, especially now. We're all supposed to be saving.'

He opened his mouth as if to protest, then closed it and again turned away. Maddie went to reassure him, but felt an added presence. She swiveled toward the window. Centered between the swooped drapes, Mrs Moritomo stood behind a white veil of gossamer curtain. The woman threw a glare before stepping out of view.

Perhaps fleeing with his family wasn't the wisest choice. Though what else could Maddie do to keep him close? There had to be another option.

Unable to think of one, she confessed to the greatest reason behind her proposal. 'Lane, I'm just so afraid of losing you.'

After a moment, he connected with her eyes. Only a tinge of sadness appeared in his soft smile. Gently, he pulled her into his arms. 'I'm sorry, Maddie,' he told her. It was all he needed to say.

She rested her head on his shoulder and inhaled the scent of his skin, like leaves after an autumn rain. She had missed this smell, this feeling, even more than she realized.

'Em!' Lane called suddenly, and broke their hold. 'Emma, what is it?'

Stifling sobs, she sprinted onto the porch. She clung to her schoolbooks as she disappeared into the house.

Lane sighed. 'Probably just another kid teasing her. You stay here, I'll be back in a minute.' He brushed Maddie's lips with a kiss, then headed inside.

Left alone, she perched on a rail. All her life she'd lived only minutes from here, yet this was the nearest she had ever been to Lane's front door. She wondered about his room. What color was his bedspread? Which treasures had he kept since childhood? What decorations adorned his walls? Assuming his mother permitted any.

At last, Lane reemerged.

'Is Emma all right?'

He held up a crinkled flyer. Sketched in the middle was a bucktoothed boy with squinty eyes mounted on a plaque, like the head of a deer, topped with a banner of neatly penned cursive. *Jap Hunting License. Open Season. No Limit.*

'Where did she get that?' Maddie said, aghast.

'A kid from school gave it to her, thought it was funny.' His tone made clear what he wanted to do with that kid, given the chance.

Maddie was searching for something to say when a cannon of slurs pelted them from the street.

'*Get out, you traitors!*'

'*Go home, Jap rats!*'

Maddie turned and spotted a red object being slung toward the house. A brick! Lane pushed her down, covered her body with his. The window

168

shattered into a downpour. Tiny shards sprinted down her arms as she breathed against the porch floor.

Victorious whoops and whistles overlapped, then quickly waned.

Lane raised his head toward the attackers. 'They're gone,' he assured her. He helped her up, brushing off her arms. 'Are you hurt?'

She shook her head tightly. Her heart was beating at a hummingbird's pace.

Around a distant corner, the gang of boys jetted away on their bikes. No older than twelve, they had already learned to hate.

Lane continued to stare after them, long after they vanished. When Maddie clutched his hand, he dropped his gaze to her fingers. 'You'd better go,' he said.

She wanted to object, but his mother had made clear Maddie was far from welcome in their home.

Neck still trembling, she kissed him on the cheek and whispered good-bye. Although the impulse to run for safety itched at her, she maintained a steady pace through the neighborhood.

Seeing her house brought a wave of relief, which ended at another sight. Her left hand. Bare of a wedding ring!

She had forgotten to move it from her necklace to her finger, as she'd always done before their visits. She told herself Lane hadn't noticed, distracted by their discussion and the vandals and Emma – but deep inside, she knew he had seen.

CHAPTER 21

What a load of bull!

TJ marched out of the locker room. He continued across Bovard Field to reach Coach Barry, intent on putting the rumor to bed.

Around him the USC players were stretching and warming up beneath the buttery tarp of sun, readying for the scrimmage. This used to be TJ's favorite time of year. Spring training. He'd loved the promise found in the scent of fresh-cut grass, the feel of tight seams on a new ball, like a clean slate in his grip. Sanded bats would whoosh in effortless arcs, his spikes would find balance in the leveled dirt, and he knew he was home.

Of course, that home was now withering. In absence of his passion for the game, the banisters dangled and stairs creaked. The pipes were leaking, warping the floors. But so long as the support beam remained, the house would stand.

That's why word about his coach's plans couldn't be true. Besides, look at the guy. He was a middle-aged family man, juggling three sports for the school. No way he was leaving all that behind.

'Coach,' TJ said, 'got a minute?'

Coach Barry held a pencil in one hand, team roster in the other. 'What's on your mind, son?' He scribbled notes in the margins as TJ debated on his approach, decided to keep it light.

'Just thought you'd get a kick out of hearing the latest, is all. Some of the guys, they're saying you up and enlisted.' He forced out a small laugh to punctuate the lunacy of the idea. Only way TJ himself would be serving was through the draft. No point in volunteering for a war due to end in a year. 'Bunch of hot air, right?'

Coach Barry stopped writing. He eased his head upward. The motion carried a reluctance that leveled TJ's smile. 'News sure spreads fast around here, doesn't it?'

TJ twisted his glove, trying to squeeze sense out of what he was hearing. 'You're not saying you actually joined the Navy?'

'Never been one for the sidelines,' he said. 'And with so many students joining up, figured I could at least do my bit by helping with training. I was planning to tell everyone after practice today.'

Within earshot, Paul Lamont was playing second base. He smirked at TJ, as though reveling in the news.

'Not to worry, though,' Coach Barry added. 'Coach Dedeaux's gonna take real good care of you boys while I'm gone. You just keep your eye on that diploma and give this season your all.' He patted TJ on the back. 'Go on, son. You're up now. Show Essick your best stuff.'

Sent on his way, mind reeling, TJ trudged toward the mound. Sure enough, seated in the stands amid scouts for the Red Sox and Dodgers was Bill Essick. The famed scout for the Yankees had discovered the likes of Joltin' Joe and Lefty Gomez. Good ol' 'Vinegar Bill.' TJ hadn't done much to impress the guy during winter league. Starting today, though, he could show all of them what he had. He could prove himself the gem they first caught a glimmer of two years ago.

Unfortunately, his arm had turned to rubber, weakened from the blow of Coach Barry's news. The more he pondered his coach deserting them – the last constant in his life – the more his feeling of betrayal swelled.

Pitching would be his vent.

Once ready, he scuffed at the mound, sidled his foot up to the rubber. Greenery draped the surrounding fence leading to a scoreboard. No numbers on it today, this being practice, but today every pitch would count.

The catcher signed a screwball. TJ cleared his head as best he could. He aimed for a look of cool and collected, then let the first one fly.

A strike. With it came no satisfaction, just the compulsion to do it again. So that's what he did. Gaining focus, he hurled one after the other. Knucklers, four-seamers, splitters, sinkers. What he lacked in control today, he made up for in power. Hard and determined he threw. His shoulder burned from exertion. His eyes stung from dust and disappointment. He didn't listen for the song inside, the one he'd lost. It wouldn't be coming back.

And who needed it? Who needed anyone, really?

Another of his teammates stepped up to bat, a new hotshot scholarship pitcher. He wiggled his spikes in place, gave a practice swing, and muttered something resembling a challenge. On another day, TJ would take the needling in stride, all part of the game. But right now, his mood demanded he stuff that cockiness back where it came from.

Fittingly, the catcher called for a slurve. When executed right, the experimental slide-curve combo created a nice weapon. An unexpected pitch to throw the guy off.

TJ channeled all of his emotions into the ball trapped in his glove. He didn't bother to visualize the path, just the rookie's humbled expression. Breath held, TJ drew back and unleashed the slurve full force. The ball swung wide, too wide, before it broke – *wham* into the hitter. His lower spine.

Shit.

Coach Barry rushed to the plate. Several players from the dugout did the same. Slowly, the batter rose from the huddle. They walked him off the field, not a single eye in TJ's direction.

'Nice one, Kern.' Paul closed in with an ugly grin.

'Get back to your base.'

'That your new strategy? Wipe out the competition?'

TJ's fingers clawed the interior of his glove as he tried like hell to ignore the weasel.

'Guess I don't blame ya. With Coach Barry gone soon, you'll be pulling slivers out of your ass from riding that bench.' Paul smacked his chewing gum around, a sound that grated on TJ's nerves like sandpaper. 'Or, you could just drop out now. Maybe join your Jap friend when they clear 'em out of the area. Hell, out of the whole country if we're lucky.' More smacking as he turned for his base.

What happened next passed in a blur. TJ didn't register his own actions until Paul was lying on the ground. The jerk scrambled to his feet and flung off his baseball cap, charged forward shouting. 'You gonna shove me from behind, asshole?'

Other infielders interceded, keeping them apart.

'Come on, you coward! I dare you to try it again!' Paul reached through the nest of limbs and grabbed TJ's sleeve. By the time TJ wrestled the grip loose, Coach Barry stepped up to mediate.

'Break it up, the both of you,' he barked. 'Lamont, go cool off in the dugout.'

Paul's wriggling stopped, but his glare remained on TJ.

'Now, Lamont!'

Conceding, Paul jerked away from his team-mates' restraining hands.

Coach Barry addressed TJ. 'What was that all about?'

It wasn't Paul's potshots that had pushed TJ over the edge. It was the fact that the guy had seen the romance between Maddie and Lane first. And worse yet, that he'd embedded digs about Japs into TJ's mind – about being liars and yellow and filthy – making the words far too easy to spit out.

'It was nothing,' TJ muttered, and straightened his cap with a tug.

Coach Barry glanced over at home plate. He shook his head helplessly. 'Better call it a day,' he said.

TJ didn't argue. And this time, he didn't bother to gauge Essick's reaction. He just tossed away his glove and walked off the field – with no intention of returning.

CHAPTER 22

The unfathomable had become reality. President Roosevelt had signed an executive order, allowing the removal of any persons from any area the military saw fit. That area was turning out to be the entire West Coast; and the people, those with Japanese ancestry.

They started with Terminal Island. Gave them forty-eight hours to evacuate. How does an entire community pack up and move in forty-eight hours? Their families and houses, their livelihoods.

For months, Lane had hidden daily newspapers from his mother. There had been no need to rattle her further. History courses had taught him that journalists with extreme viewpoints tended to represent a vocal minority. Fanaticism and fear, over evidence and reason, sold papers. When the *Los Angeles Times* had printed declarations of vipers being vipers no matter where they were hatched, he'd dismissed his budding of anger. Paranoia would run its short course, and the typewriters would shift to accurately reflect the overall sentiment of the country.

But through FDR's order, the country had spoken.

And Lane had been ruled a viper.

Seated in a far corner booth at Tilly's Diner, Lane reviewed these thoughts to gather his courage. The manila envelope lay front-side down on the table. He told himself he was making the right decision; that he was giving Maddie the needed out she would never ask for.

Still, he regretted arriving so early, allowing too much time to think. He should have chosen another place to meet. At a diner, she would be expecting a casual, lingering date.

Too late to make a change. Maddie had just arrived.

She approached the table smiling, radiant in her peach dress. He'd known her too many years not to recognize when she had put special effort into her appearance. Her hair hung long, pinned neatly at her temples. Rouge and lipstick brightened her face, spurring his urge to kiss her.

'Have you been here long?'

He shook his head. To his relief, she slid into the seat across from him; the division of the table hindered him from acting on impulse.

'I don't know about you, but I'm starving,' she said, setting aside her pocketbook.

Hamburger sizzled and scented the air. From a corner of the room, a jukebox projected 'Embraceable You' to a sparse early-lunch crowd. Autographed portraits of movie stars hung in frames on the wall. He noted all of this, not wanting to forget the place in which he and his friends – namely TJ – had spent countless hours over the years.

'Let me guess.' Maddie smiled. 'Strawberry malt with extra whipped cream.'

He was about to agree, when he recalled the purpose of their meeting, and his gut churned. 'Not today.'

Her eyes widened in exaggerated astoundment. 'Are you sure you're feeling all right?'

'Maddie,' he began, 'I need to tell you something.'

Gradually she sat back, as if becoming aware of the tension.

He cleared the resistance from his throat. But before he could continue, a navy-blue form swam into his periphery. Ruth stood at their table in her diner dress, a pencil behind her ear. She held her order pad to her chest.

Expecting her predictable greeting – *The usual, Lane?* – he interjected, 'We need a few minutes, please.'

The waitress didn't move. Her motherly features looked distraught. 'I'm real sorry, sweetie. But we have a new manager, and, well, he thinks you'd be more *comfortable* eating somewhere else. I told him you probably just missed the sign, and you weren't trying to make trouble.'

Lane lifted his eyes and discovered the back of a small poster taped to the window. He could imagine what it read without seeing the front. *No Japs Allowed*. There were plenty of the same around town, at markets and barbershops, but it hadn't occurred to him that a place he'd grown up in would subscribe to the insanity.

'I'm real sorry,' Ruth repeated with genuine care, then left their booth, exposing a view of customers' glares and whispers. Apparently he'd been too preoccupied to notice them.

'Come on, Lane.' Maddie clutched her pocketbook. 'We'll just go.' She slid from the seat and waited for him to respond.

Against the weight of humiliation he managed to rise.

Outside, they walked without speaking. They were halfway down the block, in search of an alternate spot, when Lane stopped her. There was no reason to delay the inevitable, and the gentle approach he'd planned had been whittled away.

'This is for you.'

Accepting the envelope, she said, 'What is it?'

'Us being together,' he stated simply, 'it isn't going to work.'

Her face darkened, as he'd expected. But then she discarded his claim with a shake of her head. 'We'll be fine. I told you, we can move wherever we want to go.'

'We made a mistake.' The phrase felt like metal shavings in his mouth, each syllable a tiny razor. 'It's time we faced the truth.'

'Wh-what do you mean?'

'We made a mistake,' he forced out again.

'Stop saying that!' Her eyes lit with moisture, her skin flushed.

He restrained his arms from enfolding her. 'The papers are already filled out. There's a pen inside. Please just sign them.' He angled his head away. He could hear her slide the packet out, the gasp from her mouth.

'Divorce papers?'

After an infinite pause, no pages rustling, he glanced up to confirm she was reading. Rather, she was staring at him. From the devastation in her eyes, he felt a ripping in his chest, the severing of his heart.

'Lane, please don't do this.' Her voice strained through her tears. She touched his cheek, and a slow burn moved over his skin. 'You're the only person I have left.'

He clasped her fingers, harnessing truth that would only destroy her in the end. And from behind his facade, he peered at her. 'I'm sorry, Maddie. But I don't love you anymore.'

Before his resolve could buckle, he turned and let her go.

CHAPTER 23

'C'mon. Just try a little.' Maddie heard the words through the pillow covering the back of her head. 'It's a cinnamon roll, your favorite.' Jo's gentle coaxing dwindled with her patience. 'For Pete's sake, you gotta eat somethin'. It's dang near three o'clock.'

'I'm not hungry,' Maddie mumbled into the mattress. In fact, she doubted her appetite would ever return.

A soft clink indicated Jo had placed the silverware and plate on the nightstand, where the divorce packet remained. Since receiving it yesterday, Maddie couldn't bear to open the envelope again.

The bed dipped as Jo took a seat. 'You know, Maddie, could be this is for the best. Maybe it's like that opera you told me about. Where the girl and guy are keen for each other, but they meet at the wrong time, and their worlds are just too different.'

Suddenly Maddie regretted that she'd relayed the premise of *Aida*. She needed someone to convince her that life could end happily. Like a snappy Broadway musical, not a tragic opera. Lane used to be that person for her.

Jo knew that. How could she suggest they'd be better off apart?

Lifting her head, Maddie squinted against the sunlight. 'We're *not* too different. Lane and I are supposed to be together, regardless of what others might think.'

Sure, their backgrounds varied, from finances to heritage. But they, as individuals, were the same. Their tastes in food and films were identical. During *Amos 'n' Andy* radio shows, they were always the first two to laugh. And when it came to beliefs and values, they were a perfect match.

'Okay, you're two peas in a pod.' Jo agreed so naturally, it was clear Maddie had fallen right into her trap. 'So, why don't you just go over and talk to him? Straighten all this out?'

'Because – it's not that simple.'

'Oh. Oh, yeah, I see your point. You would, after all, have to stop feeling sorry for yourself long enough to change your clothes. How long you been in this outfit anyway?'

'I am *not* feeling sorry for myself.'

'Could've fooled me.'

Maddie groaned, retreating into the pillow. She should have known better than to call on Jo for sympathy. Raised in a household of boys, the girl hadn't exactly mastered the art of coddling.

'Ah, Maddie. Forget the baloney he told ya. I mean, jeez Louise, if I ever had a fella look at me like that . . . well. He loves you for sure. You know he's only doing this to protect you. Boys are cavemen. They guard their clan. Granted, often in ways that make no sense whatsoever. And they almost always say the opposite of how they feel.'

In general, the explanation rang true, TJ being a prime example. The way he'd hold in his emotions, express them in an infuriating fashion. But Lane was an exception. He'd always been a straightforward guy. It was one of his greatest traits.

Although, given the current circumstances, anyone could act out of character, she supposed.

Maddie turned back toward Jo. Her eyes felt swollen from tears. 'Do you really think he still loves me?' She searched her friend's face for the truth.

'Yes,' Jo said with absolute certainty. 'What's just as important, though, is do you love *him?*'

Faced with the probability of losing Lane, her feelings were never clearer. 'Oh, Jo. I love him so much, I can't imagine living without him.'

'So fight for him.'

The suggestion sounded like the most obvious solution in the world. Perhaps it was. Again and again, Lane had fought for her, fought for them. If she didn't return the favor, and soon, she stood to lose him forever. But how?

She ran a finger along the side of the manila envelope. The document to end their marriage awaited her consent. What if she refused? He couldn't divorce her unless she signed the papers, could he?

This was her decision to make too.

Mouth set with determination, Maddie kicked off the covers. She'd had her fill of being guided by others, based on what they felt best suited her. It was high time she took hold of her own future. She began by sifting through her closet and grabbed the mint-green sundress. The color of spring, to reflect a fresh start.

'What do you think?' she asked, holding the garment up to her body.

Jo's lips curved into an approving smile. 'I think he's going to love it.'

Answer, answer, answer . . .

Maddie stood at the Moritomos' front door. With each of her steps to reach their house, her strength had gained volume and momentum. Her energy filled the porch. She felt ten feet tall.

About to knock again, she opted for the bell. She rang it twice and with purpose. Today, she had the confidence to persist even if Mrs Moritomo opened the door. Maddie was prepared to wait for hours until Lane arrived should he be out – the cinnamon roll was enough to tide her over.

'Somebody answer,' she urged quietly.

Still no one.

She rose up on her toes to peek through the arched glass in the door. The foggy pane distorted her view. Lane had mentioned that his mother scarcely left since his father's arrest. Maybe the woman had spotted Maddie through the peephole and was pretending not to be home. Or . . .

Could the FBI have returned? Taken the whole family in for questioning?

It was a ridiculous thought – Emma being eight.

Then Maddie noticed a paper taped to the window, covering the hole from a thrown brick, reminding her that anything was possible.

Anxiety rising, she strained to see through a narrow opening between the closed drapes. She could make out a mere sliver of the floor. No movement. Below the patched hole, she discovered a wider view. Her hand cleared a circle on the dusty glass. The couch was gone. And the coffee table. The whole formal room appeared empty.

At the shop, she'd heard mortifying tales of people walking straight into Japanese American homes and taking what they pleased, knowing the families were too afraid to call the police. Had the Moritomos, too, been robbed?

'Hello! It's Maddie. Hello!' She tried the knob. Unlike most houses, it was locked. Sifting through possibilities of what had happened, she rushed to the next-door neighbor's. She pounded on the door with her fist.

A plump Mexican woman poked her head out. 'Yes?'

'I'm sorry to bother you, ma'am, but I think burglars may have broken into the Moritomo home. All of their things – we need to call the police.'

To Maddie's dismay, the woman didn't dash to the phone. Her features simply drooped, their sullenness explained through words that cracked the sky.

'The family moved away.'

CHAPTER 24

How was it possible? Plenty of food in the pantry and yet TJ couldn't find a single thing to eat. This always seemed the case anymore. Reaching for things he couldn't have. An appetite for what he couldn't see, couldn't identify.

Flicking the last cupboard closed, he heard footsteps in a rapid climb of the stairs. He hollered up, 'Maddie? Have you seen the tomato soup I bought?' Quick and easy, it was better than nothing. He hadn't eaten anything since his breakfast of stale Butter Horns on campus.

'Maddie?' he yelled again. A door upstairs slammed.

Oh, boy. Now what?

Given their cordial exchanges over the week, he couldn't imagine being the cause of today's annoyance. In fact, he hadn't talked to her since yesterday morning on his way out.

He went upstairs, rapped on her door. The sound of dresser drawers opening and closing projected from inside. Concern drew him into the room.

He watched his sister skitter about. Her hair

hung haphazardly from her twisted-up do. Dried tears streaked her powdered face. She snagged blouses from her bureau and tossed them into a suitcase on her bed.

'Where are you going?'

At the closet, she tore through the hangers. She was moving on a different plane, where no one else existed. Garments slipped off and landed in puddles of fabric. She grabbed two skirts and a dress, added them to the chaos of her luggage.

'Maddie, stop.' He raised his voice to break through, then closed his hand around her wrist. After a reflexive tug, she stilled. Her eyes raised, brimmed with pain. Before he dared to ask what had happened, she fell into his arms.

'He's gone,' she said. 'Lane's family. They sold everything and . . . just left.'

The news hit like a spitball to the chest. It's what TJ had wanted – what he'd asked for, even – but somehow he didn't see it coming.

He rubbed his sister's back. 'It'll be all right,' he repeated over and over. Each time he tried to sound more convincing. Her fresh tears soaked through his T-shirt, though it was guilt that stung his skin.

'Where could they have gone?' she said as if to herself, which explained her packing frenzy.

'Maddie, you can't go off chasing them around the country. They could be anywhere. If it's meant to work out with you and Lane, it will. After the war maybe.' He couldn't believe what he was suggesting.

'They couldn't have gone far,' she concluded as she straightened. She was solving, not listening. 'His father. How could Lane leave with his father still away?'

'His dad'll be fine,' TJ insisted. 'Lane said it was only a formality. I'm sure he'll be back with his family soon.'

'But how will he know where . . .' As her question trailed off, she took a step back. 'When did Lane tell you that?'

'When did – what?' he stammered, catching himself too late.

'You talked to him,' she realized.

TJ avoided her eyes. Nonetheless, he could sense her viewing his memories; his confrontation with Lane was replaying like a scene in a picture show.

'It was you,' she said.

'Maddie . . .'

'*You* did this.'

'Now, just hold on. Listen to me.' He reached out, but she jerked away.

He anticipated a furious outburst. Instead, her reply came slow and molten. 'Get . . . out.' The two words screamed with finality.

Then she turned toward the window, arms hugging her middle, and stared with the bearing of a stranger.

'Another one!' a drunkard yelled from the other end of the bar from TJ.

The bartender took the liberty of pouring the

man a coffee, told him it was spiked with booze and on the house. He then stopped in front of TJ. 'Problem with the drink, pal?'

Ordering a shot of whiskey had seemed a fresh solution, to drown his troubles, if only for a night. Everything else had failed. Since the accident, he'd steered clear of anything except an occasional beer. But why? Drink or not, he'd be damned if he became his father.

'The whiskey's fine.' To prove it, TJ threw back the shot. Liquid heat hurtled down his throat and flamed his chest. 'The same,' he rasped.

Towel slung over his shoulder, the bartender refilled the glass. TJ didn't waffle over this one. He had no reason to. For the first time since he was a youngster, he had no coach demanding he keep his nose clean, no parents setting the rules. Just a sister who believed he was ruining her life. Which maybe he was.

The alcohol swished around in his stomach. Without food in there for padding, he already felt a light sway of his barstool. He envisioned himself on a raft, air seeping from a hole. He was scrambling to plug the leak, but another puncture appeared, and another. The holes expanded until he realized he'd been patching them with a knife, and nothing would keep him from sinking.

'Can I settle the check?' a guy nearby asked the bartender. In response, the man nodded and started tabulating on his order pad.

'Kern, right?'

TJ turned to the customer. Tall and skinny. Looked familiar.

'Eugene Russell,' he said, indicating himself. 'We have Management class together. Or had, I should say.'

'Why, you drop the course?' TJ's question stemmed not from interest in his classmate, but from a desire to do just that. Way things were going, he'd have to work like a hound to skim by with a passing grade.

'My buddies and I are enlisting today. Just stopped here for a bite to eat on the way.' Across the room, a group of three preppy college boys rose from their table, putting on their jackets.

'Good for you.' TJ returned to his empty glass, ready for a refill.

'Six-fifty,' the bartender announced.

The tall kid produced seven crisp bills from his wallet. 'Keep the change,' he offered with pride, then said to TJ, 'Take it easy. Oh, and good luck with the season.'

Yeah. The season.

'Thanks.'

The guy rejoined his friends by the table. Smiles plastered their faces, a sign of purpose gleaming their eyes. How nice to have a purpose, to get out of this city and start over. Someplace where your history, your mistakes, weren't hunkered around every corner prepared to pounce.

TJ motioned to the bartender for another shot, though it was the last thing his stomach wanted.

What *did* he want? He wished he knew. Those guys heading for the door, they knew what they were after. Had a future ahead guaranteeing respect. Parades. Medals. Gold stars and glory in death. He could almost hear the regal notes of 'Taps' playing on a horn, could see the pomp of a folded flag.

The scene suddenly had appeal.

'Russell, wait.' His voice flew out, swinging the kid around. Before TJ could think twice, he let the next words fall. 'I'm coming too.'

PART III

A sparrow flew in amongst a group of happily playing quiet waterfowl and disturbed the peace. For the sake of the pond's peace the young sparrow will leave and fly away.

– Okumura Hirofumi
excerpt from a farewell letter to his lover

CHAPTER 25

Rolling onto the graveled lot, the Buick digested its last sip of fuel and choked to a stop. Lane gripped the steering wheel, palms sweating from dreaded awareness: The dusty filling station in front of him, eight miles from their latest motel, was his family's final option. His hunt for gasoline had stretched past noon, winding him through the small Texan town planted south of the New Mexico border.

With his unpolished shoes, he brushed aside Hershey's wrappers on the floorboard – remnants from Emma's snacks during their cross-country drive – and stepped out of the car. The tang of diesel struck harder than the untrusting eyes of a middle-aged couple seated in their pickup truck. A shotgun hung on the back window of their cab.

Lane made his way toward the station attendant. The freckled teen, skin blotched from the May sunlight, was swiping his forehead with a rag when he froze.

'My tank's empty.' Lane gestured to his car, which appeared as worn as he felt. 'I'd like to fill it up if I could.'

The kid didn't respond at first, stuck in deep fascination, as if a Martian had just landed and asked to refuel his ship. 'I – uh, sure – awright.'

It wasn't until Lane absorbed the words, and balked at the guy's agreement, that he realized how little hope he had sustained. 'Thank you,' he said. He stopped himself from volunteering the number of times he'd been refused gas during their trek from L.A. to Santa Fe. Now en route to the detention center in Crystal City, supposedly his father's most recent transfer, their luck hadn't been much better. Maybe things were turning around.

'Would you mind giving me a hand to bring it closer?' Though wary of asking for too much, Lane would need help rolling the vehicle over to the pump.

'Yessir.' The kid followed him, then spread his hands on the rear of the Buick.

Lane opened the driver's side and prepared to push while steering. 'Ready?'

A man's holler interrupted. 'What're you doing there, Junior?'

'Just movin' this car over, Pa.' The kid righted himself, his shoulders still hunched. 'Fella's outta gas.'

'You leave it alone now,' his father ordered. Streaks of oil stained his mechanic's jumper. Beside him, the customer from the truck stood with hands hitched on his trousers, watching. 'You heard me, Junior. Go on, now.'

As the kid stepped away, Lane felt a bubbling

of emotion. 'Please,' he said to the mechanic, 'just give me some gas and I'll happily leave.' While intended as a plea, the words came out with a gruffness he didn't intend.

'Sorry, can't help ya here.' The man sounded anything but apologetic. 'Have to take your business elsewhere.'

Lane spoke as calmly as he could through gritted teeth. 'How am I supposed to take my car anywhere? Tank's completely empty.'

'Reckon that's your problem to solve, now, ain't it?'

The customer at the man's side slid a glance to his gun rack. Inside the pickup, the woman gripped the dashboard. Fret filled her eyes. In that look, Lane saw it all. Through a distorted lens of fear, implanted from Pearl Harbor, his crime was unforgivable. Even worse than murder, he had stolen their security. And eliminating the thief was a sure way to recoup that loss.

Lane showed them his palms, a sign of surrendering. He walked backward several paces, the tension waning with distance. At the border of the lot, he turned and started the long walk toward the motel.

'Hey, fella,' the kid called after him. 'Don't you want your keys?'

He gave the single response they all wanted from him.

His silence.

★　　★　　★

'*Onīsan!*' Emma threw her arms around Lane the minute he returned. 'Where have you been? You were gone so long.'

He hugged her back, and for a moment, any troubles that existed outside their dingy rented room scattered beyond care. 'Sorry, Em. It just took a bit longer than I thought.'

'*Onaka ga*—' His mother spoke from a corner chair, then began again. 'We hungry.' Her tone verged on a scolding, but Lane felt no offense. The worry that creased the edges of her eyes betrayed her veneer.

He pulled on a smile. As head of the family, the solution was his to find. 'Let me clean up and we'll go get some food.' He crossed the room, the bedding as threadbare as the mud-colored carpet. An odor resembling an old attic stretched into the bathroom, where unseen mold heaved its mildewy breaths.

Door closed, he splashed water on his face. Rust ringed the sink. He let the drops trail off as he stared into the mirror. His face had aged five years. A whorl of hair fanned upward, confused by the absence of Brylcreem. His white buttoned-down shirt was tinted with dust from passing cars; that, and more than two months of rotating through the same suitcase of clothing.

He went to the toilet, its sound of running water a nuisance, and retrieved his Mason jar from the tank. Coins tumbled against a thinning cushion of dollar bills. Their cash savings wouldn't last forever. That's what he'd told Maddie when she had proposed they run away.

At the thought of her, a string of memories rose into view. He could see the two of them at an aquarium, laughing as they fed the barking seals. He saw a folded note stamped with a lipstick mark that she'd slipped into his coat: *Missing you.* He had found it while on his train ride to Stanford at the start of fall. That's what the season had been – a steady fall from the life he'd known. One Maddie didn't need to suffer.

'You made the right decision,' he said firmly to his reflection.

He almost believed it.

Glancing around at the chipped tiles, the window too small to escape through, he reassessed their mission. Hunting for their father served no purpose other than to keep them moving. Even if the man was indeed in Crystal City when they arrived, then what? Seeing him would be out of the question. A receptionist at the Santa Fe detention center had explained that repeatedly, encouraged them not to waste the effort.

And how would they get there – by bus? How many more motels would refuse them rooms? How long before they were denied passage? Residents at several state borders were said to be blocking eastbound Japanese attempting to resettle voluntarily.

No state wanted to be California's dumping ground, a columnist had reported.

Lane rotated the jar in his hands. *Clink, clink, clink.* Bargain hunters had bought their appliances and furnishings for five cents on the dollar. *Clink, clink, clink.* A green portrait of Thomas Jefferson peered from a two-dollar bill. Lincoln's profile shone bright in bronze. These were the faces that represented the America he knew, the men who fought for freedom and equality. The very values that defied racial internment.

Still, under their leadership, their worthy causes had required sacrifice. Maybe Lane ought to accept his own duty, no matter how wrong it all seemed. Besides, what else could he do? Evacuation of the West Coast's Japanese was in full swing, and jobs would undoubtedly run scarce for a man with slanted eyes. Highlights of the relocation centers, on the other hand, included occupations and newly built housing, recreational activities and schools.

Emma needed to be in school. She needed to be with other kids. According to a spokesman, ten camps had been established to protect, not punish, more than a hundred thousand of Japanese heritage. Lane had discounted the claim as a guise, but perhaps truth lay within the propaganda.

God, he missed his father. Nobu Moritomo would know what to do.

A knock on the door turned him. 'Onīsan, I'm staaarving.'

He clutched the jar and opened the door. Emma looked up at him with eager eyes. He tenderly squeezed her chin, praying he was about to do the right thing. 'We'll get something to eat,' he promised her, 'right after we pack.'

'I thought we weren't going to Crystal City till tomorrow.'

'We're not going to Crystal City anymore.'

'Then, where are we going?'

Lane met his mother's puzzled gaze before he answered. 'Back home.'

CHAPTER 26

From the urgency of Bea's entrance, Maddie tensed for disastrous news.

'Lordy, Maddie. You won't believe it. You simply won't.' Bea panted as she closed the shop's door. 'Oh, sugar, watch the iron.'

Maddie lifted the appliance from a customer's pleated skirt in the nick of time.

'Just let me catch my breath.' Bea fanned herself with an envelope from the counter. An intentional delay, it seemed. What could have gone so wrong to give her second thoughts about relaying her discovery?

Oh, no – TJ. He must have been wounded. Could word travel faster through conversation than a telegram? He was still only in training with the Army Air Corps, but accidents occurred all the time. He could have been shot in a misfire at gunnery school.

Maddie had told him she agreed with his enlistment, after her initial jolt. Told him that giving each other space would be good for them both. But she hadn't expected how hollow the house would feel, amplifying worries over his safety. Nor how challenging it would be to maintain a cool distance in their letters, which she suddenly regretted.

'Tell me what happened,' Maddie said to Bea. *Get it over with.*

'It's Mrs Valentine. She was at the nursing home today visiting her aunt. I just happened to bump into her outside my husband's office while I was droppin' off his lunch. You remember Mrs Valentine, don't you? She used to make those Christmas wreaths your daddy always bought to raise money for the Girl Scouts.'

Maddie shook her head *no*.

This couldn't be about TJ. Regardless, she was hesitant to relax.

'Well, we got to chatting about the shop and what have you. Turns out, she'd heard all about your playing the violin for your daddy, and about your not going to Juilliard on account of – well, due to the war.'

A gentle way to put it.

Maddie almost asked how Mrs Valentine had caught news about her financial and marital predicament, but then, who in Boyle Heights hadn't?

'So then,' Bea said, moving closer, 'she tells me how her brother-in-law plays for the symphony up in San Francisco, and how he owed her a favor for something or other. Naturally, I told her you'd be grateful if there were anything he could do. And much to my surprise, she marched straight over to the phone and dialed him up. O' course, she didn't go into a whole lotta detail with him – men get all flustered from too much information – and well, he tells her there should definitely be entrance scholarships available from the school.'

Maddie was well aware of that option. What she didn't know was how to respond without drizzling on Bea's parade. Maddie had never heard the woman carry on with such excitement, her pace contending with that of Mrs Duchovny. Or rather, the Mrs Duchovny people more fondly remembered.

'He's right,' Maddie gingerly affirmed. 'They don't give out more than a handful, though. And once you're accepted, you have to audition for the scholarship in person, in New York, just days before the term begins.'

The scenario seemed unendurable: scraping together money for application fees and travel fare, while towing a year's worth of clothing in an over-sized trunk, only to be informed she couldn't attend.

'Yes, yes,' Bea said. 'But apparently, it helps to have a faculty member's recommendation. He says that if the person listens to you play and speaks on your behalf, presuming you're good enough – which heaven knows you are – your chances of a scholarship increase by leaps and bounds.'

This still did nothing to help Maddie's situation, or her somberness. For weeks, she had been distracting herself with extended hours at the shop. As if sewing shears could trim away the jaggedness of Lane's departure and the frays of her father's dream.

'Bea, it's splendid of you to do this for me. I'm terribly grateful. But I don't know a single person on the Juilliard staff, and I don't suspect I'll be meeting one anytime soon.'

'You, my dear, have a month.'

A month . . . 'For what exactly?'

'To practice. You see, it just so happens that Benjamin, Mrs Valentine's brother-in-law, is an old acquaintance of Mish – Mishnauff,' Bea stammered. 'Oh, bother, how did she say it?'

Recognition bristled Maddie's posture. 'Mischa Mischakoff?'

'Ah, good! You know of him.'

Maddie had heard the Ukrainian violinist play a recital years ago, and the magnificence of his performance, the tonality he controlled as it flowed from his Stradivarius, still reverberated in her ears.

'Here's the thing, sugar,' Bea continued. 'He has a trip planned to San Francisco. Benjamin will be hosting his visit, and is sure the man would be delighted to give you a private audition. As Benjamin's guest, he could hardly say no, now could he?'

Assembling the swirling pieces, Maddie asked, 'Mischakoff is teaching at Juilliard?'

'Newly added, I believe they said.'

'But how did – Benjamin couldn't have spoken to him yet.'

'No, but he gives his word, and Mrs Valentine

claims that's good as gold. You just need to mosey on up there, prepared to show your stuff.'

An audition for Mischa Mischakoff. Was it possible?

Maddie's hands flew to her cheeks, pulled by an urge to keep her grin from floating to the ceiling.

Then she considered the time line.

'Did you say a month?' Four weeks never seemed so short.

The grin that slipped off Maddie's face had transferred onto Bea's. 'I'd say you'd best get busy.'

'But, a month . . . I haven't been keeping up like I should have.'

'Then I suggest you stop lollygagging and get to work.'

Audition pieces swam through Maddie's mind as Bea handed over a sweater and purse, and shooed her out of the store. Maddie turned around, remembering. 'Are you sure? There's a pile of alterations waiting, and more ironing to be done.'

Bea shook her head, fists on her hips. 'Seeing where your head's at, you'll be useless to me anyway. Hems going this way and that. Iron burning holes clear through. Now, go.'

Maddie threw her arms around the woman before following the order. 'Your father would be so proud,' she thought she heard Bea say. Then she realized, yet again, the words had come from within.

As the bus rumbled toward home, Maddie didn't feel a single bump. Her body levitated over the seat, her surge of joy like a magic potion. She couldn't wait to share the news with TJ and Jo and her father – whether her dad showed outward signs of hearing didn't matter today. But most of all, she was dying to tell Lane!

Seized by reality, her heart plunged into a free fall. Too late she recalled the danger of permitting happiness to raise her spirit to such heights. The higher the jump, the more destructive the landing. She brushed the thought away, and froze at the sight. An Oriental woman was seating herself six rows ahead.

Maddie would swear the passenger was –

Mrs Moritomo?

From the back, the woman's figure appeared identical. Familiar pearls encircled her dainty neck. A comb adorned with sparrows, Kumiko's favorite bird according to Lane, secured a smooth black chignon.

Nonsense. She couldn't be Lane's mother. They were gone. Across the country by now.

Yet Maddie watched her, unable to move. The bus paused at one stop, then another. Passengers got off, got on. They rocked in unison, tilted around corners. Finally the woman rose – for the approaching stop that used to be Lane's – bolstering Maddie's excitement.

When the vehicle squeaked to a halt, Maddie joined the line to exit. Her gaze clung to Kumiko, the key to locating Lane. Could his family be staying in their old place? Changed their minds, turned the car around? Twice Maddie had gone to their house, just to be sure, and found it vacant. A sign on the door: *For Lease.*

Treatment in other towns might have been worse. Their father could have been released, prompting their return. . . .

Possibilities multiplied until the Japanese woman turned to de-board. Her profile revealed her age to be thirty at most. With a narrower face than Kumiko's, rosier cheeks, and a higher bridge of the nose, she looked Chinese, not Japanese. Assuming *Time* magazine's comparative illustrations held any validity.

Either way, she wasn't Mrs Moritomo.

Maddie sank into the nearest seat, her hopes kicked out from under her. The bus rolled onward, as did her thoughts until settling on Juilliard. She pictured the application, its signature line as black, solid, and blank as the one for her divorce. Countless times she had stared at Lane's petition, even hovered a pen over the pages. But a thin thread of faith had kept her from signing. A thread that now fully unraveled.

The instant Maddie entered her house, she headed for the document she could no longer avoid. She refused to mull over what she couldn't change, no matter how much she'd always love Lane. Instead, with divorce papers in hand, she said good-bye through a sting of tears. And she signed her name.

CHAPTER 27

TJ waited for the target with his finger on the trigger. He braced his hip against the circular rail mounted on the bed of a pickup, the butt of the twelve-gauge snug into his shoulder. The truck bumped and rattled beneath his boots as it rounded the track. Behind him sat two privates who'd finished their turns. Now they were tasked with keeping score and feeding ammo.

Another clay pigeon soared from the trap. TJ followed its arc and fired, bursting the disk into fragments.

In his mind, that one was Paul Lamont.

A few guys here at gunnery school had asked TJ for the secret to his accuracy, his hits being unusually high. His answer was truthfully simple. 'Picture the enemy.' He just never elaborated with specifics. Better to let them assume he was referring to Nips or Krauts, not enemies closer to home. Paul had easily become his favorite target, followed closely by his father and Lane. Sometimes TJ himself.

The vehicle slowed after the final curve. TJ wasn't quite ready to give up the relief of moving air, nor the activity that passed the hours, but what choice did he have?

He relaxed his grip, lowering the shotgun. Thanks to the Vegas sun, the metal barrel could cook a Western omelet. Man, an omelet sounded like paradise compared to the mutton stew they served for chow. Between the sorry meals and sweat marathons, he hadn't been this lean since junior high.

With a rag from his uniform trousers, he mopped his neck and forehead. 'Dry heat, my foot,' he muttered.

No one deserved to be stationed in a barren wasteland like this. But at least he'd left the humidity of Keesler Field far behind. Basic training in Mississippi had ended not a day too soon.

The truck pulled over to the entrance, where the gunnery sergeant coordinated skeet shooting. 'Gotta take a leak,' Sarge told the driver, and strode away.

A small cluster of Air Corps privates waited to board. As always, Vince Ranieri stood at the helm. He wore his Italian smile like his black wavy hair, slick and suave. His magnetic confidence drew in just about everyone – except TJ.

'Save any ammo for us this time?' the guy scoffed.

TJ set down his weapon, though he suddenly found it tempting to hold on to, and climbed down with the others. He headed for the barracks without responding.

'C'mon, Kern. Don't tell me you're still sore over me tanning your hide.'

Muffled snickers leaked out from the group, slowing TJ's feet. Consistently, when it came to the top spots, he and Ranieri had been neck and neck since first arriving at the airfield. From aircraft recognition to turret maneuvering to air-to-ground firing.

In the machine-gun drills, however – disassembling a .50-caliber and putting it back together – TJ had yet to have his time bettered by a classmate. Till this morning.

'I wouldn't celebrate too much,' he flung over his shoulder. 'Even a busted watch is right twice a day.' More snickers from the bystanders.

'Ahh, so it was sheer luck,' Ranieri said. 'You sure about that?'

The whole scene felt too much like a repeat of TJ's last scuffle at the baseball field.

''Cause if you're sure, real sure, maybe you'd like to put some money on it.'

TJ told himself to keep walking, to ignore the dope. A few swings and they'd be tossed into the greasy pits of KP duty.

'What do you think, fellas? Surfer boy lost his stuff?'

Whether it was the excess of heat and testosterone in the air or being challenged before an audience, TJ's patience evaporated. He swung back around and caught eager anticipation on the other gunners' faces. In the middle of the desert, it didn't take much to constitute entertainment.

'So what'll it be, Kern?' Ranieri pressed. 'Ten bucks on tomorrow's drill?'

TJ leveled his gaze at the smirking Italian and shrugged. 'Why wait?'

Remarkable how fast news could spread about a pissing contest. That's basically what the hoopla amounted to, a stupid kids' game, but TJ's competitive streak made it impossible to back down.

In a training building, stocked with machine guns, he and Ranieri prepared for battle. They stood at opposite ends of a waist-high table, their M2 Brownings poised before them. A circle of three dozen airmen created a makeshift arena; all traded shouts of numbers, a mix of odds and dollars, with the gusto of a title fight at Madison Square Garden.

Next came blindfolds. TJ imprinted a fresh image of the machine gun in his brain. When the cloth blackened his vision, he released a long exhale. He pumped the stiffness from his hands and wrestled down the possibility of losing. With equal effort, he pushed away the ever-present thought of *What the hell am I doing here?* For a whiskey-glazed minute, enlisting had seemed the best way to care for Maddie. In spite of her recent assurances, he still questioned his own judgment.

Especially now.

'Pipe down,' a guy bellowed at the room. 'Let's get on with it. You boys know the rules. No shortcuts, no cheating, and the fifty-cals gotta fire to count. On your mark . . . get set . . . go!'

TJ was off, starting with the barrel group. One piece at a time, riding the border between speed and precision, he worked to disassemble the weapon. He removed the backplate. Pulled out the driving spring assembly. Took the bolt from the receiver and proceeded without a hitch.

Once he'd completed disassembly – halfway there! – he immediately charged into reversing the steps. A cough from someone off to the side reminded him he wasn't alone. The whole air base seemed to be holding its breath.

Concentrating, he replaced the barrel buffer assembly. He paused only to swipe his palm on his shirt. Collective body heat was intensifying his sweat. With the notch joined on the shank, he aligned the breech lock depressors. He snapped the spring lock and secured the parts and told himself not to rush. He was picturing the clearance hole when the bolt stud slipped from his fingers. *Damn it!* Blindly he fumbled for the piece. Following the sound of rolling metal, he recovered it next to the drive spring.

He couldn't panic. Just had to get back on track. He continued through the steps and heard Ranieri struggling with the retracting slide handle. TJ still had a chance. He unscrewed the barrel two clicks. The finishing line within grasp, he removed the link, closed the cover, and declared his win with a—

'Done!' Ranieri shouted.

A throng of cheering voices sucked the air from TJ's chest. Nothing like having your pride walloped in a public forum. Exactly what he needed, a demonstration of another shortfall.

TJ ripped off his blindfold as the ringleader shushed the mob and said, 'All right, Ranieri. Let's see it.'

With an arrogant grin, the guy replied, 'My pleasure.' He laced his fingers and cracked his knuckles to gear up for the formality. After all, he had yet to fail a function check.

TJ turned away, itching to scat before salt could hit the wound, just as Ranieri went to pull the trigger.

But it didn't click.

His face fell as he yanked harder.

Still no sound.

Half the room burst into celebration.

'Now, let's not get ahead of ourselves,' the announcer warned. 'Gotta make sure yours is in working order, Kern.'

Ranieri stared at his machine gun, clearly stumped by where he'd gone wrong.

TJ felt the jolt and dip of a mental roller coaster. He readied his weapon for the test. Bolt latch released, he rode the bolt forward and placed his finger on the trigger. *Please work, please work.* And he pulled.

Click. The tiny sound was as beautiful as an ump yelling, 'You're out!' at an opposing runner, sealing a win.

In the hustle and bustle, greenbacks transferred pockets. TJ stepped away from the table, almost giddy from the trivial upset, and found himself face-to-face with the competitor. Grimness had replaced the Italian's boastful glee from only moments before. Was he looking to go to blows?

TJ rolled his hands into discreet fists. But instead of a punch, he received two folded five spots. A nice surprise. He had to give the fellow credit. Ranieri was a far better loser than he himself would have been.

As TJ started away, Ranieri piped up. 'So you gonna sport me a beer at least?' His signature grin had returned in full force. TJ couldn't help but smile back.

'I thought you meatball types only drank wine.'

'Wine on Sundays, my friend. Beer every other day of the week.' He offered a handshake, which TJ accepted, and by the third round that evening, in different ways it seemed both of them had triumphed.

CHAPTER 28

Lane didn't know what he'd been expecting, but it wasn't this. He walked through the eerie stillness, his tweed cap pulled low, and turned from San Pedro Street onto First. Shadows spread over the block like an almighty hand. The hustle and bustle of pedestrians, the scent of udon broth, the ringing of bicycles and hollers of beckoning vendors – all were gone. Little Tokyo had been gutted.

Signs on building exteriors and in every window told a story. *Going out of business. Everything half price. For sale. Sold. Closed. We hope to serve you again. I am an American.*

For as long as Lane could remember, he had preferred to shop elsewhere. He'd chosen Sid's Drugstore over Nippon Pharmacy, Leaders Barbershop over Nakamura's. He had compiled reasons for the superiority of each. But perhaps the real basis of his favoritism had stemmed from nothing more than the quality implied by their 'all-American' names.

Judging by the streets around him, a ghost town of his heritage, his view hadn't been unique. Thankfully, his father wasn't here to see this.

Just then, a silhouette moved in Ginza Market. Lane looked closer. Nobody there. A mere reflection from the retreating sun. Where would he find a snack for Emma?

He had ventured out of the Buddhist temple, his family's temporary shelter, on an errand for his sister. Her eyes had told him she wanted to tag along but understood that remaining with their mother took priority.

Mochi cakes, Emma had requested. Aoyagi Confectionery made her favorite of the glutinous rice balls filled with sweet red beans. He'd agreed, wanting to distract her from concerns over their destination, some camp in the state's eastern desert. Rumors of the place had circled like mosquitoes, nipping away, swelling fears of deportations and forced farm labor. They described roving coyotes and scorpion infestations, families separated and traded for American POWs. Mass executions if Japan invaded the mainland. All preposterous.

Or not.

Propelled by the promise to his sister, he continued down the empty street. He stepped on scraps from wooden crates. He followed the trail of crinkled flyers. The same proclamations were posted on utility poles.

INSTRUCTIONS TO ALL PERSONS
OF JAPANESE ANCESTRY

Forcing the exodus of an entire race from an area had become disturbingly efficient. The pages detailed where and when to report, what they were and weren't permitted to pack.

At least Lane's family didn't have to worry about the limitation of bringing only what they could carry; that's all they had left. Little more than essentials remained after shedding items for their long bus ride back to California. Sunny Southern Cal, with its sandy beaches and lush palm trees. Where imagination bloomed and hope streamed in the sunlight.

Of course, none of these could be found in the confines of the temple's basement. In a time not so far back, Lane's mother would have griped plenty over their creaky squeezed-in cots, the mix of body odors from strangers varied in caste. But not now. And her silence, outside of one- or two-word answers, bothered him more than her complaining ever could.

Lane paused to review his surroundings. His feet had steered him to the last place he would have chosen. Kitty-corner from Kern's Tailoring. Miles of aimless walking hadn't been aimless after all. He wasn't wearing his watch – he'd hawked that too – but was certain the lights inside were shining for Bea. Maddie would be home, making supper for herself and TJ. Meat loaf and creamed corn, or a chicken casserole with Green Goddess Salad. Those were the dishes she had made when Lane used to join them.

At her absence now, disappointment flowed

through him, but also relief. Seeing her would only make matters worse. Only tempt him to retract the lie he had told her.

'Holy Toledo. I don't believe my eyes!'

The familiar voice swung Lane around. In a khaki Army uniform, Dewey Owens was exiting Canter Brother's Deli. The last contact from the guy had been a brief but supportive note. He'd mailed it with Lane's belongings from the dorm.

'Good to see you.' Lane smiled and accepted an outstretched hand. A friendly face was never so welcome.

'I can't believe you're in town. Thought you and your family were zooming around the country.' Dewey made it sound as though they had been off on a whirlwind vacation, a road trip on a whim.

Lane was trying for a simplified answer when two GIs emerged from the restaurant. They looked on with unreadable expressions.

'Fellas! Let me introduce you.' Dewey sped through their names, and all exchanged hand-shakes and nice-to-meet-yous. Then the two soldiers backed up a few paces, lighting their Lucky Strikes. Lane would like to think they were merely giving the old roommates space to catch up, but who knew anymore?

'What're you doing out here tonight?' Dewey asked.

'I was just looking in on a friend.' Lane's chin inadvertently motioned toward the tailor shop, causing Dewey's eyes to follow. No chance taking the gesture back. He tried distracting with small talk, but the guy wasn't listening.

'So *that's* the dream girl. . . .' Dewey grinned, sly as an alley cat.

Leave it to him to make a crack about ogling Beatrice. Lane went to sling a retort – the guy's colorful love life had produced an ample amount of dirt – until he glimpsed the store window. There, Maddie appeared inside. She was hanging garments on a wall hook, balancing the fabric, picking off lint. His breath hitched at the sway of her auburn hair, the memory of feeling the silky strands on his skin.

But then he recalled what had happened since, that those times were over, and . . . that he'd never told Dewey about their courtship.

'How did you know?'

'About Maddie?'

Lane nodded.

'I was your roommate for almost four years, buddy. You think I'm *that* oblivious?' He gave Lane's upper arm a pat. 'Do I get to meet her or what?'

Lane peered at the woman behind the glass. 'She doesn't know I'm in town,' he said. 'It's better that way.' Slowly, he tore his focus from her. 'So you're an Army man, huh?'

Dewey shrugged. 'Put me in Intelligence, if you can believe it.'

'And they still expect us to win?'

'Guess they were smart enough not to give me live ammo.'

Lane smiled, and for an instant, he envisioned himself in the same uniform – but only an instant. Even if the U.S. military weren't turning away Nisei, his patriotism had depleted too much to volunteer.

'Owens, we're gonna split,' said one of the soldiers, flicking his cigarette butt onto the sidewalk.

'I'm coming.' Dewey turned to Lane. 'We're hitting some bars on Wilshire. Come out with us.'

Lane considered the invitation. He appreciated any enticement to draw him from the temptation across the street. Then he spied a policeman in the distance meandering in their direction, and the invisible bars of curfew and travel restrictions returned.

'Actually, I'd better get back. We have to report to St Timothy's by nine in the morning for evacuation. So . . .'

Dewey's face tightened, a mixture of sympathy and wanting to beat a fistful of sense into someone. But he simply said, 'Take care of yourself.'

'You too,' Lane offered with equal sincerity.

They shook hands good-bye, then Dewey followed his friends around the bend.

Lane slid his hands into his jacket pockets. He glanced at the storefront once more, just as Maddie clicked off the first set of lights. Closing time. Before she turned off the second, he raised his collar around his ears and headed toward the temple. Empty-handed, nothing for Emma. Another promise broken.

CHAPTER 29

Engines awoke in the distance, a stagger of roars that cinched Maddie's throat with panic. Her pace doubled in speed. Her leather heels clicked a staccato rhythm on the city sidewalk. She forced air in and out, in and out, against the burn crawling up the walls of her lungs.

Nine o'clock, that's what Lane's roommate had said when the operator connected his call that morning. Told her that his conscience wouldn't let him ship off without at least telling her Lane was in town, but if she wanted to see him, she had until nine o'clock.

She'd raced out the door. No time to think.

At last, she was almost there. . . .

A young soldier stood up ahead. He hugged his bayonet-fixed rifle across his chest, his stance undoubtedly fresh from Army basic. He stared hard into the sky, as if reading his mission etched in the ribbon of clouds. *The enemy, have to protect our country from the enemy.*

The thought curled Maddie's fingers.

In a glance briefer than a blink, the GI sized her up, her ivory skin an armor of presumed innocence. She swerved around him, not missing a beat. To her left, personal effects awaited transit in a snaking queue. Cribs and ironing boards, labeled trunks and boxes. Their tags dangled in the spring sun.

Around the corner, evacuees were amassed before the steepled church. Red Cross volunteers handed out coffee.

'Lane! Where are you?' Her words died in the bedlam, smothered by a baby's cry, a rumbling jeep, a little girl's hysterics.

'But I don't want to go,' the girl shrieked, face stained red. 'Mommy, I want to stay with *you!*' Tears streamed from the slanted eyes that cursed the child, dripping trails down the puffy sleeves of her lilac dress. Two nuns pried her fingers from the Caucasian woman's arms and guided the youngster toward the bus.

'Everything will be fine, pumpkin,' the mother choked out against a sob. 'Mommy and Daddy will come see you soon.' A suited man beside her added, 'You be a good girl, now.' His Anglo features contorted in despair as he limply waved.

A reporter snapped a photo.

Who knew a piece of paper could carry so much power? One presidential order and an orphan could lose another family; one signed petition and marriage vows could be unsaid. Thank God she hadn't mailed the papers yet. Stamped and sealed, but not mailed.

Maddie scanned the faces around her, their

223

features similar to Lane's, but none as flawless. None bearing the deep beauty of his eyes, his smile.

'Lane!' she shouted louder. The trio of chartered buses was filling. Within minutes, he would be gone.

'Excuse me, miss. May I help you?' A priest touched her arm. His wrinkled face exuded warmth that penetrated the morning chill.

'Moritomos – I have to find them.' Exhaust fumes invaded the air, causing her to cough.

He patted her back. 'Now, now, dear. Let's see what we can do.' They wove through the crowd, her gaze zipping from one figure to the next. Beige identity tags hung from lapels, around buttons. Branded in their Sunday best like a herd of cattle.

'Sergeant,' the priest called out. He stepped up to a bulky Army man in the midst of lecturing two privates. 'Sergeant,' he tried again, 'I hate to interrupt, but . . .'

'Hold your water,' the guy barked, before turning and noting the source. His shoulders lowered. 'Sorry, Father. What is it you need?'

'This young lady, here, she's trying to locate a particular family.'

'The Moritomos,' Maddie cut in.

The sergeant sighed heavily as he lifted his clipboard. He flipped forward several pages and began his search through the list. With the top of his pen, he scratched his head beneath his helmet. He blew out another sigh.

This was taking too long.

Maddie leaned in, trying to see the smudged names herself. *Maeda . . . Matsuda . . . Minami . . . Miyamoto . . .*

The sergeant turned to the next page and looked up. 'What's that name again?'

She fought to keep her composure. 'Moritomo. Lane Moritomo.'

A loud hiss shot from behind. The first bus was pulling away, followed by the next. Another hiss and the doors slammed closed on the last Greyhound in line. The crowd launched into waves of farewells and see-you-soons, whenever, wherever that might be.

'Maddie.' A muffled voice barely met her ears. It came again, stronger. 'Maddie, over here!' Someone yanked open a dusty windowpane on the remaining bus. It was Lane, reaching across seated passengers to see her.

She wasn't too late!

Calling his name, she bumped through elbows to get to the blue-and-white striped transport. She scrambled for his hand until their grips linked, his skin soft as a glove. When a smile slid across his face, all else paled to a haze. Time reversed, back to happier days, before the ground had crumbled on a fault line, dividing their world in two.

'I didn't mean what I said,' he implored, 'at the diner. . . .'

'I know,' she assured him, for it was a truth she had carried inside. Still, her heart warmed from the confirmation in his eyes.

Then the bus began to move.

'No matter what happens, Maddie, know that I'll always love you.'

She tightened her grasp, refusing to let go. 'I'll be waiting. However long it takes.'

On the balls of her feet she hastened her stride. She struggled to keep up, but the wheels were spinning too fast. Against her silent pleas, their connection wouldn't hold and his fingers slipped beyond reach.

CHAPTER 30

Entering the room was even harder than TJ had expected, and the sight more alarming. Hunched in a ladder-back chair, the robed man stared distantly out the window. His profile resembled little of the father TJ remembered. Graying scruff lined his jaw. Wrinkles created a road map of time and tragedy.

TJ dropped his duffel bag on the rest home floor. Garrison cap in hand, he took a step forward, then another. The clicking of his polished shoes on tile didn't prompt a reaction. His father's blue eyes held on a summer sky of the same shade.

TJ reached for an adjacent chair, but changed his mind. He wouldn't be staying long.

'Dad, it's me.'

Nothing. Just staring.

He tried again, louder. 'I said, it's me. TJ.'

On the train ride home that morning, he had contemplated this moment. The 'delay in route' supplied his last chance to confront his father before deployment. If nothing else, he ought to say good-bye. In case.

'I know you probably can't hear me, but . . .'

He cleared the rasp from his throat and straightened in his uniform. The shiny gunner's wings surely would have made his old man proud. Not that TJ cared. Why would he anymore?

'I just came to tell you that I'm shipping out soon, and I thought . . . I thought that . . .'

He rubbed a hand over his buzz cut, running low on words but heavy on memories. Snippets of his past assembled in a collage: his mother's seven-bean stew that once won a ribbon at a local fair; little Maddie following him everywhere, close as Peter Pan's shadow; his parents cheering from the stands after TJ's first no-hitter; and at the center of the images, his last camping trip with his father before college began. They'd lounged around the campfire, sipping their pungent coffee. Croaking frogs and chirping crickets had provided a backdrop to their comfortable silence.

So many moments. Now all irrelevant.

Here, in this structured enclosure, nature's sounds gave way to the squeaking of rubber soles and rolling carts, the clinking of metal trays. Each sound depicted movement with purpose. Of passersby in the hallway driven by the needs of others.

Faced by the contrast of his father's world, one of mere existence, TJ felt sympathy form low in his chest. It expanded like a bubble as he studied the room. The framed dime-store prints, the narrow bed, its solitude folded into Army-tight corners.

Then a thought returned. He'd sworn he would never forgive his father. Sworn it with everything in him. From that recollection, the sphere of sympathy popped, pricked by a needle of blame.

'Mr Kern,' a nurse said, entering. 'Time for – oh, pardon me. I didn't mean to interrupt.'

'I was just leaving,' TJ told her, to which she gave a reassuring wave.

'There's no hurry, dear. I was fetching him for his afternoon walk. Are you a friend of the family?'

'No,' TJ said, before adding, 'He's . . . my father.'

'Oh, I didn't realize he had a—' She stopped herself and smiled uncomfortably. 'How silly of me. I should've seen the resemblance. Well. Feel free to take your time. I'll swing by later.'

'No need, ma'am. I have to go anyway.' He turned to his father, and without meeting his eyes, he bid a quick good-bye.

TJ recognized the tune but not the voice.

He set his duffel and tunic in the entry of his house, and followed the lyrics of 'Boogie Woogie Bugle Boy' toward the kitchen. August had warmed the hall by a good fifteen degrees since the day he'd left, yet more than the temperature felt different.

The scent of a baking dessert piqued his curiosity, pushing out reflections on his father, and drew TJ closer to the singer. In the kitchen, she stood with her back to him.

Jo Allister . . . he should have guessed. She belted

out an off-key high note that made him smile rather than cringe.

Arms folded, he leaned a shoulder against the doorframe. Her bound hair bobbed like a buoy as she diddel'd and yada'd about a Chicago trumpet man playing reveille. She sponged the tiled counter in a circular motion that matched the beat of her swaying hips. Nice sway actually. *And* nice hips. Her typical outfits were hand-me-downs from her brothers, hiding what now appeared to be an attractive figure. Her tan pedal pushers hinted to as much, even if her baggy button-down shirt, knotted at the waist, didn't. Which was a real shame, since –

TJ bridled the rest. This was Jo, the equivalent of another sister. Not to mention Maddie's best friend. Striking up more than friendship would verge on hypocrisy, considering his view of Lane. Besides, at this point, nothing good could come of a romance with anyone.

'You're home,' Jo exclaimed in mid-turn. Her bronze eyes lit with delight, before the spark blew out. He could see her recalling their last encounter, the full bucket of anger he'd dumped on her. 'Maddie said you weren't comin' till tomorrow.' Her altered tone implied she had planned to be somewhere else. Anywhere else.

'I was released from the base earlier than I thought.'

'Mm.'

She gave his uniform a quick glance that showed

no sign of being impressed, then retreated to the sink. Heat from the oven radiated through the room.

Setting his hat aside, he wiped his forehead with his sleeve. 'So how've you been?'

She scrubbed her hands with soap, hard, not addressing the question. 'Maddie should be back soon. She's delivering clothes to a neighbor on Fairmount, for the stamps she got.'

'Stamps?'

Jo sighed, annoyed. 'They made a trade. Maddie mended some trousers for ration coupons, 'cause she didn't have enough sugar. And she wanted to bake you a cake.' Under her breath, she added, 'Though only God knows why.'

Boy oh boy, Jo was a tough nut. Oddly, though, he found her even more likable after seeing her in a huff. 'So, what kind of cake you got there?'

'*Devil's* Food,' she said after a pause.

'Ah, yeah? My favorite.'

'Yeah, I know—' The sentence caught. She grabbed a plaid dish towel and dried her hands. 'Since you're here now, *you* can keep an eye on the baking. Just pull it out when the bell goes off. It's flour-less, so it'll be denser than usual.' She set the towel on the counter and walked past him.

'Come on,' he said. 'Don't rush off.'

'Got stuff to do.'

'Jo . . .' He trailed her toward the entry, led by a growing need to keep her there. He hadn't realized how much he'd missed their talks, or just being with her, till now. 'Jo,' he said again.

But she flat-out ignored him. Her hand made it to the door handle when he blurted, 'I saw my dad today.'

It was enough to halt her.

Slowly, cautiously, Jo faced him. She waited for him to continue.

'Figured I should . . . with me shipping out on Sunday.'

She nodded, disdain dropping away. 'How'd it go?'

'Fine, I guess. Doubtful he heard anything, but I said what I needed to.'

A shadow of a smile lifted the corners of her lips. 'That's good.'

In the quiet stretch between them, it dawned on him that she'd never had the chance to say good-bye to her own dad.

'Well, I'd better get,' she said. 'Your sister's gonna want some time with you.'

'Jo, listen. Before you go . . .'

She waited again.

If he couldn't right things with his father, he should at least make the effort elsewhere. 'I wanted to say that . . . that I'm sorry, for blaming you about Lane and Maddie. I was angry, and, well, it wouldn't have been right for you to stick your nose in. So . . . I'm sorry for putting you in the middle.'

Jo arched a brow. 'Wow. Two sorrys in a single day,' she mused. 'How'd those feel coming out of your mouth, airman?'

'Rough enough to chip a tooth.'

'In that case, apology accepted.' When she grinned, he couldn't help but laugh.

'Seriously,' he told her, 'why don't you stay. If you helped bake the thing, you ought to enjoy a piece.'

'What makes you so sure I helped bake anything for you?'

The smudge of cake batter on her cheek gave her up. He walked over and gently swiped the evidence with his thumb. He meant to withdraw his fingers, but to his surprise, found he couldn't. The softness of her skin held them in place. He looked into her eyes, and a feverish charge shot through him, sending a bead of sweat down his spine. His mind said to step back, but his body acted on its own. He watched his hand venture to her neck and her mouth slightly open. Her breath smelled of cocoa, her hair of lemon. He leaned several inches closer, wanting to taste the sweetness dusting her lips, when he heard a click.

The front door.

He shifted away with the speed of a rifle drill. 'Maddie,' he said.

His sister's eyes widened – from his return, he hoped, not the scene. 'TJ, you got in early! You should have wired me. I would've met you at the station.'

'I – wanted to surprise you.'

Maddie returned his smile. But then her lips relaxed as she glanced at Jo, whose skin had gained a shade of pink. Maddie's attention bounced back to him with an air of suspicion. 'Am I interrupting . . .?'

'What, us?' He scrunched his face, motioning to himself and Jo. *She's one of the guys,* he said without saying it. 'I was only walking her out.' An uneasy pause.

'Yeah,' Jo said coolly. 'I was just leaving.'

Unable to meet Jo's eyes, he tossed her a 'see ya,' and headed for the kitchen.

What the heck was he doing? Months of training with an assigned bomber group would do this to any fella, right? Too much time spent in the barracks. Too many postcards of pinup gals or chats about one broad or another. With the amount of testosterone packed into their B-17, it was a miracle they'd made it off the tarmac.

At the sink, TJ downed a glass of water that wasn't nearly cold enough. He refilled it as Maddie entered the room. Dodging an inquiry, he gestured to his uniform. 'Whaddya think of the getup? Not too shabby, huh?'

She shook her head at him. A skeptical look, he assumed, until she spoke. 'I can't believe you made corporal already.' Her face warmed with pride.

Too bad the pride was unwarranted. In his view, he hadn't earned the rank more than any other private. 'Don't let the stripes fool you. Just luck of the draw.'

'Oh, I highly doubt that.'

He didn't respond, simply drank his water. Why dim her glowing opinion?

'So . . . ,' she said, a prompt that dangled. With nowhere to go from there, the conversation hovered over unwritten words in their letters.

TJ preferred to concentrate on what had actually appeared on those pages. Six months of postal exchanges had helped fill the cracks in their relationship.

'So,' he parroted as his sister checked on the oven. 'Give me the dope. What's the latest round here?'

Maddie tucked her pageboy hair behind her ears and leaned back against the counter. 'Well,' she said, thinking. 'I did receive a nice note from Professor Mischakoff. He invited me to play for him again, once I get to New York. Sort of a final polish before going in front of the panel.'

'Does that mean you got confirmation from the school, that they've given you an audition slot?'

'They did.'

'And what about the application for the scholarship?'

'It's taken care of.'

'Filling it out, or mailing it?'

'TJ.' She reached over and touched his sleeve. 'I've got it handled. Really, I'm not a little girl anymore.'

Despite the maturity she'd gained while he'd been away – more definition in her cheeks, more curves to her sundress – she was still his baby sister. Always would be.

Skirting a debate over the point, he charged on. 'And what about the shop? Business picked up any?'

'A little. Lately most of the alterations are just to make old clothes last. But it's all for the war effort, so we can hardly complain.'

He was going to ask about managing the store, since they'd both be away soon, but then Maddie added, 'Bea has assured me over and over she'll have everything under control. Combined with your Army pay, the bills are covered. And Jo will be checking on the house.'

Had his nagging become that predictable?

TJ grinned in spite of himself. Tension inside him loosened, a settling into the familiar.

In a casual tone, Maddie continued, 'Lane's family is doing all right, by the way, in case you're wondering.'

The run-in with Jo had thrown him off. Otherwise, he'd have been better prepared for this subject. He would have noticed, before now, the wedding band on his sister's finger that solidified her stance.

'I'm glad to hear that,' he said, a reflexive reply he immediately regretted. He didn't mean to cause the flicker of hope in her eyes.

'I'm planning to go see them soon,' she said. 'By train, it's only about five hours away. I keep asking in my letters, but Lane told me they don't allow visitors yet.' She paused and lifted a shoulder. 'I was thinking, if you're back here on furlough sometime, maybe . . .'

These, he recognized, were the unwritten words. He knew what she wanted in response, but as much as he loved his sister, he couldn't give it to her.

In the wake of his silence, she dropped her gaze to the counter. As she scraped her thumbnail at a dried spot of batter, he realized she might have the wrong idea.

'I want you to know,' he told her, 'I don't necessarily agree with what's been done. Driving the Japanese from their homes, putting them into camps. Just because I can't forgive Lane doesn't mean I think it's right.'

She raised her head. 'But, why *can't* you forgive him? You've forgiven me, haven't you?'

'That's different.'

'How?'

'You're my sister.'

'And he was a brother to you.'

'Maddie, stop.' He rubbed the back of his neck in agitation. But soon, calming himself, he forced out a sigh. What harm would there be in giving her an inch? 'Listen. When the war's over and he comes back, and if you do end up staying together' – which hopefully wouldn't be the case – 'we'll sort through everything then.' He finished gently, 'Till that happens, let's enjoy the time we've got before I ship out. Deal?'

With a thoughtful nod, she offered a smile. 'Deal.'

The cooking timer rang, a welcomed interruption.

Maddie clicked off the dial, and TJ handed her a potholder. He breathed in the heavenly wafts of chocolate as she retrieved the metal pan from the oven. His mouth salivated, starved for better food than Army chow.

'Damn – I mean, dang, that looks good.' Again, too many hours with airmen and no ladies present. 'Let's dig in.'

'Hold your horses. We have to let it cool first.'

'No way. I ain't waiting.'

'But you'll burn your tongue.'

'A small price,' he said, pulling a fork from the drawer.

'TJ Kern, don't you dare eat out of the pan.' After a roll of her eyes, she conceded by reaching into the cupboard for plates. 'Some things never change,' she muttered with a small laugh.

Though TJ kept it to himself, he disagreed.

Everything was changing.

CHAPTER 31

'You don't know what you're talking about!' The guy shot up from his wooden bench at the mess hall meeting. Lane recognized him as a kitchen worker. A Nisei in his late twenties, he wore a thin mustache, a rarity among their community at the Manzanar camp.

'Then why don't you tell us what's happening to our block's sugar?' another fellow demanded. The roomful of seated Japanese men murmured their agreement. 'You saying our supply's been walking away on its own two feet?'

'I'm saying you better think again before you accuse our crew of stealing.'

Listeners fanned themselves with magazines, sheets of paper. The evening temperature sweltered. Lane had to consciously contain his urge to speak, his collegiate council days over. No good would come of intervening here, he'd learned. After ratcheting up, the meeting would land on its circular tracks. A repeat of arguments would roll out from every corner.

The War Relocation Authority thought it a favor to allow self-government, but achieving cohesion

239

was no simpler than finding a needle in a sack of rice. From immigrants' dialects to cultural diversity, residents of the fourteen-barrack block differed in every way save one: the ancestry that had sentenced them to this desert wasteland.

Tonight, as usual, it didn't take long for the guys from Terminal Island – with their shogun-like attitudes and rough fisherman's language – to make their opinions known. They wanted better meals and higher pay for jobs, improved medical treatment in the understaffed, undersupplied camp hospital. And they wanted someone to blame.

'I say we get the whole camp to boycott meals,' one guy announced.

'That's genius,' a man behind him sneered. 'Let's starve ourselves. I'm sure the *hakujin* officials will come running.'

'You got a better idea?'

'Yeah. How about you JACL'ers learn to shut your mouths for a change? You're the reason we all got sent here in the first place.'

More *here-we-go-again* grumbles. More guys brought to their feet. After two months of these gatherings, Lane wasn't quite sure why he attended at all. Except, he hated to admit, for the slim possibility of making a difference.

A lean kid with glasses stood up, a seasoned debater. 'The JACL,' he said, 'has done nothing but defend us as loyal Americans. What would it have said if we'd protested? Everyone in the country is doing their part. And when the war's over we'll have erased any doubt of us being the enemy.'

That was as far as he got into his spiel, delivered as a devout member of the Japanese American Citizens League, before his opposition chimed in. Once more, they revived the tired dispute of the organization being in cahoots with the FBI, even prior to the attack on Pearl Harbor.

The block manager started tapping his gavel. He didn't cease until the group quieted. At the semblance of order, he called upon an elder at the end of Lane's row, who rose to impart reasoning.

'*Shokun, sukoshi kikinasai,*' he began, but a Nisei interrupted.

'Speak English, old man. You know that Japanese isn't allowed at meetings.'

The suited gentleman was taken aback. Although he carried a humble, dignified countenance – not unlike Lane's father – he clearly wasn't accustomed to taking orders from one so much younger. And frankly, Lane wasn't accustomed to watching it. Filial piety, values embedded since birth, dictated respectfulness that propelled Lane now from his seat.

'*Shikata ga nai.*' He hadn't planned to spout his father's phrase, but it flew out all the same. *Shikata ga nai. It can't be helped.* One couldn't walk past four barracks without hearing an Issei recite the saying. Same for their reminder of the reason to quietly persevere. *Kodomo no tame ni.*

For the sake of the children.

241

'Regardless of what brought us here,' Lane told the room, 'we're in this together. We need to stop wasting time by fighting. We need to find solutions.'

The sea of men's heads nodded in agreement, reigniting a familiar flame, though small, in Lane's chest. He faced the rows behind him, gaining momentum. 'If the kitchen crew says they're not taking the sugar, then I for one believe them. We have to trust each other. If we want to solve the problem, we should take the matter up with Director Nash. Maybe start with beefing up patrols at the warehouse.'

'*Kuso!*' The word *bullshit* boomed from the doorway, where three members of the Black Dragon gang glared with arms crossed. These particular Kibei, Japanese Americans who'd spent much of their lives in Japan, had channeled their anger over internment into a mission: to promote loyalty to the Emperor, through violence if need be.

Lane turned away from them and continued. 'What I'm saying is, we'll make more progress if we organize our approach. Remember, this was how we succeeded at the net factory. Last month, when we asked for—'

'No!' shouted one of the Dragons. A small scar cut through his left eyebrow. 'Only way to make *hakujin* listen – this!' He smacked a fist into his other hand. 'You want know who steal sugar? *Hakujin* who work camp. White people. They take warehouse food and sell on black market. And *inu* helping them!'

Whispers through the mess hall grew like static. Paper fans fluttered faster.

'*Inu* like you maybe?' The same gang member pointed at the JACL defender. 'Or *you*.' His finger angled at Lane, who gritted his teeth at the accusation.

Being called an *informant*, a traitor to his own kind, topped the list of insults. His father remained in a detention center for the simple fact that he wasn't a rat – for either side. He was a loyal American, as was Lane. And the real *bullshit* lay in every syllable vomited from these lunkheads' mouths.

Lane couldn't hold back, his honor at stake. He moved toward the Dragons, all three now descending upon the room. They incited feuds with challengers, mainly the fishermen with no qualms about going to blows.

Then a hand touched Lane's chest. It was the elderly man in his row, warning him with a shake of his head. Without speaking, he communicated the reason for restraint.

Kodomo no tame ni.

For the sake of Emma, for the sake of his family. To keep them safe.

Lane took this in, unclenched his fingers. His duty came first. Once more he tucked away his pride, and forced himself to turn around. Voices rose as the gavel rapped, and Lane ducked out of the room.

On the bumpy dirt road, gravel crunched beneath his scuffed shoes. The ever-present wind whipped off the Sierra Nevada, howling along with unseen coyotes. He raised the collar of his shirt against the flying sand and blinding searchlight. The beam followed him as he made his way toward the paltry unit that had become his family's home. Each 'block' contained matching tarpaper barracks and a full set of community buildings. Latrines, laundry, recreation and mess halls. Clever residents gave their barracks names like 'Little Tokyo Hilton' and 'The Dust Devil Inn.'

Come to think of it, Lane was wrong. Manzanar evacuees had more in common than bloodline; they had the alkaline dust. It invaded their food, their hair, their clothes. Warping of unseasoned lumber caused knotholes and cracks that invited inches of the blessed stuff into their 'apartments.' Like every conversation, every cough or baby's cry, it traveled through their dividing walls and raised flooring. It moved like a ghost, left trails thick as lies.

The one saving grace? Complaining about the dust meant not talking about the guards. It meant avoiding acknowledgment of the barbed wire that framed their one square mile of existence, or the machine guns perched on sentry posts, their barrels facing into the camp, not out.

Of these things, naturally he would make no mention to Maddie. For while he didn't regret calling out to her on evacuation day, he would continue to shield her from his ugly new world. In letters, he would tell her about camp baseball games and gardeners planting flowers and Emma learning to twirl a baton. He would write about getting his mother to try a painting class, a great feat after weeks of her stubborn solitude. And only on occasion, to explain grime on his stationery, would he mention the dust.

At the entry stoop, Lane glanced through the window of his family's unit, a twelve-by-twenty with the barest of essentials. No carpet on the planks. No Sheetrock on the walls. A single light-bulb hung from a splintery beam. When they'd first moved in, he told his family, 'Think of it as camping, but in a wooden tent.'

Emma had agreed. His mother said nothing.

Those attitudes hadn't changed, illustrated now by the usual scene. Emma knelt on her cot, playing jacks with their assigned roommates, a mother and a daughter who was roughly Emma's age. Lane's mom sat on her mattress, striped ticking stuffed with straw. Though she stared into her open Bible, the look in her eyes placed her somewhere far away. A place of lavish comfort. No doubt, in an ancient city across the ocean.

For the first time in his life, Lane understood the appeal.

CHAPTER 32

Life was becoming an endless requiem of good-byes.

Maddie had chosen to trade parting words with TJ at the house, rather than at Union Station. Watching his train pull away that morning would have been too much to bear.

It was the thought of losing yet another loved one that now brought her to the rest home. She treaded her standard path, down the tiled hall. She held her violin case to her chest. Her emotions were jumbled and in need of order, and who better to tame them than Johann Sebastian Bach.

'Sugar, aren't you gonna say hello?' A voice from behind.

In a staff uniform, pushing a cart around the corner, was Beatrice Lovell.

'Sorry, I didn't see you,' Maddie said. 'Are you working here on Sundays now?'

'Just for the day. Laverne's replacement couldn't start till tomorrow, so my husband asked if I'd lend a hand.' Bea laughed, adding, 'I suppose he was scared he'd have to launder the sheets himself.'

Maddie smiled as they continued walking

together, until news of the staffing change sank in. A stranger tending to her father's private needs made for an unsettling thought. 'Will Laverne be coming back here?' She prayed Bea meant to say 'substitute,' not 'replacement.'

'So long as we got a spot available, I imagine it'd be hers. All depends on when she's done at the camp, I'd say.'

Right then, a tall man approached Bea, identifying himself as the nephew of a resident. While they discussed a medication, Maddie's mind seized hold of the word *camp*. No longer did it refer merely to Girl Scout outings, or family weekend adventures by a creek.

Once the man left, Maddie asked, 'By camp, do you mean . . .?'

Bea nodded wistfully. 'The one up in Wyoming. Not where your husband's family is staying, I'm afraid. Otherwise, sure as rain, I'd ask her to report back with an update.'

'But what is she doing there?'

'Don't know specifics. Just that it's a hospital job at the relocation center.'

A hospital job . . . for a white woman . . .

The information began weaving into a curious shape, one with promise. Visitors weren't allowed at Manzanar, but they might be hiring. 'Do you know if the camps are filling other kinds of positions?'

Bea replied as they resumed their walk, 'I've heard about them needing teachers. For high schoolers, I do believe.' She stopped. Lips pursed, she peered at Maddie. 'Sugar, I know how anxious you are to see Lane and his family, how worried you must be. But I gotta think, at least for now, music school is where you belong.'

Not at an internment camp for Japanese. While unspoken, the implication was there.

'You'll have to make up your own mind, I suppose, without your folks having their say.' Bea patted Maddie's shoulder. 'Just give good thought to whatever you do, is all I ask.'

With that, she left Maddie alone – at her father's door.

So far, nothing about their encounter surpassed the norm. As Maddie prepared her instrument, her father's attention remained on the window. Today's visit, however, was destined to end differently. At long last, she would present the Chaconne. It was the one favorite of his she'd neglected to learn – until Lane revived the piece in her memory. She could still smell the bouquet, could feel his hand holding hers as they exchanged promises of forever.

Maddie hastened to raise the bow. Months of drilling the composition, of perfecting her phrasing, had led to this moment. She wouldn't let emotions sabotage her efforts.

Tick. Tick. Tick. The reliable metronome obliged in her head. Shutting out all but the goal, she played in simple triple time. Ingrained notes promenaded through their basic harmonic scheme. Slowly she dealt them out, too slow. The image of Lane's smile slipped in between the measures. She pushed him away and focused on the melodic lines, the shifts between soprano and offbeat bass.

Yet more memories persisted: Lane lying beside her, their limbs tangled in the sheets; his eyes darkening and disappearing as the blue bus drove away. She attacked the strings with ferocious intensity, determined to override the past. But the visuals kept coming, of life and death, happiness and despair. She saw Emma and TJ, her mother and father.

Bach's chords slurred in her head and the metronome lost its pace. A sound trumped the movement. A sob. The sound had come from *her*. Arms too weak to continue, she lowered her bow and sealed her lips. Deep inside, the cries sang on. Salty moisture reached her mouth as she collapsed onto her knees.

Her father scarcely blinked.

She had come here bearing the Chaconne, a last hope to reach him through the wordless language of music. For hours upon hours she had practiced the movement, played long after her fingers had begged her to stop.

Now, what she had envisioned to be her greatest triumph had been unmasked as a failure. Not for the unfinished performance, but the undeniable futility. No matter which concerto she perfected – she could master each and every one – still he would not hear her. He had traveled too far to reach. Just like Lane. . . .

No, she thought suddenly.

Not like Lane. For him, it wasn't too late.

She gazed up at her father, and the dullness in his eyes sealed her decision. She would not stand by again, merely waiting for the return of someone she cherished. Even if, in the end, Lane didn't come back, at least he wouldn't go it alone.

CHAPTER 33

Clock ticking, a twinge of dread set in. TJ knelt on the platform of Union Station, rummaging through his duffel bag.

'All aboard!' the conductor hollered as gruff and loud as a baseball coach.

While getting his shoes shined, a final touch to his pressed uniform, TJ had tossed his ticket into the bag. It couldn't have fallen out, could it? Doggone it all, he had to find the thing. With the long lines in the station, no way could he get a replacement in time. And the next train to San Fran wouldn't depart for several hours. He scrambled his hand in and out of his packed khakis.

Passengers continued to board, thinning the crowd. Through open windows on the locomotive, servicemen and sweethearts exchanged farewells. Mothers blew kisses and waved their handkerchiefs. Children twirled little flags like holiday sparklers. It was a scene from a parade on the Fourth of July, featuring a float TJ was about to miss.

'Blast it,' he said, and dug deeper. Rowdy flirtations streamed from a gaggle of sailors inside the train. They sliced through his concentration. But then his fingers brushed the corner of something. He yanked out a small paper. His ticket!

He issued a sigh, cut short by the sight in front of him. A pair of legs rivaling the slenderness of any pinup's. His gaze traced the woman's stockings, from the red heels to a matching dress. Its snugness showed off her shapely curves and explained the persistent catcalls.

'Lose something, Corporal?'

Sunlight created a halo around her short-brimmed hat. Steam from the steel transport floated around her. She'd pass as angelic if not for the devilish temptation of that red-wrapped figure.

'Sure thought I did, miss,' he answered, rising. The remainder of his thought vanished at her familiar features. Not with the rouged cheeks and cherry-glossed lips. Not with the hair draped long with the scent of styling lotion. But past all that, he would have sworn she was . . .

'Jo?' he said.

She confirmed his guess with a smile.

'Wh-what are you doing here?'

She placed a white-gloved hand on her hip, as if in a practiced pose. 'I came to see you off, silly. Why else?' Her voice had gained the sultry tone of Gene Tierney. In fact, everything about her now resembled the starlet.

'But, you look so . . . different.' He tried to keep his eyes on her face, yet the shock of her firecracker figure fought for priority.

'All aboard!' The conductor's warning boomed, followed by encouragement from the sailors.

'Plant a smooch on her!'

'Don't be a schmuck!'

'Give her something to remember you by!'

Jo blushed, same shade as when he'd nearly kissed her at the house. More than a few times since, he'd caught himself envisioning that moment play out. Now was his chance.

He could see her waiting. The train was waiting. Their audience was waiting.

Succumbing to the pressure, he leaned toward her. Her eyelids lowered in acceptance. But something – nerves, uncertainty – veered his lips from hers and onto her cheek. 'Bye, Jo.'

He snagged his duffel and swung toward the train, an attempt to avoid any hurt in her eyes. And he succeeded.

At the coach's entry, however, a rush of emotion stalled his foot from boarding.

'Hey, airman.' Drawn by Jo's voice, he turned to find her a breath away. 'You forgot something.'

Swifter than a blazing fastball, she placed her mouth on his. The act stunned him in place. He couldn't break away even if he wanted to, which he didn't. His eyes closed and his arms wrapped around her waist. The Navy men cheered wildly as her fingers laced behind his neck. He pulled her in closer. Warmth from her body, from those curves of hers, coated every inch of his skin. He kissed her deeper. The electrical current he'd felt at the house paled in comparison to the charge now shooting through his body.

Finally, he came up for air. It was then, peering into Jo's eyes, that he saw the girl beneath the rouge, the one in overalls with a nice pitching arm. The one who knew how to push his buttons and to make him think.

The girl he had fallen for.

Powered by the revelation, he went to kiss her some more when she stopped him with two words. 'Your train.'

He struggled to decipher her meaning. The syllables seemed foreign.

'TJ, your train,' she stressed.

The locomotive was slowly chugging away. Servicemen onboard laughed from their open windows, yelling at him to move his ass. Instantly sobered, he gave her a final peck, then took off in a sprint. He extended his arm and grabbed hold of a handlebar. Following a heave of his bag, he leapt onto the step.

He leaned out, once secure, and raised a hand toward Jo. She didn't wave back, but he could see her grinning long after the station became a tiny dot.

TJ rode the high of their parting for five full stops. Then, as it always did, fear crept in, implanting thoughts he couldn't dismiss. Thoughts like, if fate stayed on its usual path, what chance would they have at happiness? And, most important, could either of them handle losing more than they already had?

CHAPTER 34

Maddie's entire future hinged on this performance. She rehearsed the appeal in her head, feeling pressure akin to taking the stage. The buzzing over her skin, the restlessness of her fingers.

Seated in the reception area of the Civil Control Station, she started to cross her legs, then thought better of it. She had to look her best today and couldn't risk smearing the makeup-drawn seams down the back of her legs. Granted, she was all for rationing – particularly when nylon was used for airmen's parachutes – but that didn't stop her from missing her last pair of good stockings.

A man two chairs away grumbled as he flipped through the *Examiner*. Headline after headline, all about the war. Allied ships torpedoed by U-boats, a RAF night raid on Düsseldorf, an Eighth Army victory against Rommel's forces in Egypt. It was difficult to remember what had filled those articles before America's day of infamy.

Again, Maddie regarded the clock on the wall. She layered her hands over the pocketbook on her lap to still her fidgeting. She noticed the shortness of her nails and hard-won calluses. They were the marks of a musician, unfeminine traits she had never been fond of until this instant. Today they just might work to her advantage. Testament to her experience.

'Mrs Moritomo, please.' The receptionist surveyed the room. 'Mrs Moritomo?'

It took Maddie a moment to recall the name was hers. 'Oh, yes.' She jumped to her feet. 'That's me.'

The thickness of the woman's glasses magnified her surprise.

Maddie found the look disquieting, then reminded herself the reaction would soon be customary. If, of course, the impending meeting went as planned.

'I'm afraid Mr Sanborn has had a family emergency,' the gal reported. 'So he won't be able to meet with you. I'd be happy to reschedule your appointment for the sixteenth, however, if you're available.'

Sixteenth? That was two weeks away! The very thought was unbearable.

'I can't,' Maddie blurted.

'I see. Well, I won't have another opening until—'

'Please,' Maddie pleaded. 'Is there any other supervisor I could speak with? It's regarding . . . a family emergency of our own.'

The receptionist's gaze held on Maddie's face, studying her, clearly intrigued. Finally, she said, 'Very well.'

Maddie sighed. 'Thank you.'

Following the woman through the bustling office, Maddie smoothed her suit jacket and adjusted the belt. Ringing phones and tapping typewriters crowded her ears. Her eyes darted from stenciled doors to a large U.S. map. Colorful triangles hung from several states. Relocation centers.

The gal paused at an office door and poked her head in. After a brief mumbled exchange, she turned to Maddie. 'Go on in.'

Stretched to her full height, Maddie proceeded into the room.

A stout gentleman stood before an electric fan set on the metal secretary. Warm air from the open window flailed his loosely hanging tie. He lit the pipe between his teeth. His wreath of hair was blacker than shoe polish.

'Good afternoon, sir. I'm Madeline Mori—'

'Have a seat, have a seat.' Genially, he flicked his hand toward the visitors' chairs. He puffed musty-smelling plumes into the confines of his office.

Maddie sat down. She clasped her ring finger for inspiration, and waited anxiously to continue. The man moved in slow motion. He wiped his forehead and neck with a rolled rag like a person of eighty rather than forty.

'Jiminy Cricket,' he groaned, 'this heat's for the birds.' He twisted his head toward her. 'I was born and raised in Washington. The state, not the capital. Rains so much up there, when the sun comes out people think it's an alien ship.'

She proffered a smile. The second he perched on the edge of his desk, forcing her gaze upward, she restarted. 'Sir, as I was saying . . .'

'Please. Call me Dale.'

'Madeline,' she replied in turn. His friendliness struck her as rather informal for a first meeting, particularly with an administrator at a government agency. But she needed him on her side. 'Sir – or Dale, rather – I've come to ask about applying for a position.'

His eyebrows popped up. 'Is that so? And what sort of experience do you have? Shorthand? Typing, I presume.'

Realizing his assumption, she clarified. 'Not for the office here. I'm a violinist. Since I've heard the camps are hiring teachers, I wanted to offer my services as a music instructor. Specifically, I'd like to work at Manzanar.' Wary of coming across too bold, she added, 'If at all possible, that is.'

'Manzanar, huh?' He sounded befuddled she had even heard of the place. He took another pull from his pipe.

Perhaps her credentials would help.

'I've been professionally trained for more than ten years. Naturally, I'd be happy to play for someone to prove my qualifications.' She should have brought her violin along. Why hadn't she thought of that?

He shook his head, mopped his neck. 'That won't be necessary.'

Worried by what that meant, she pressed her

case. 'I have people I care about there, which is why I'd like to lend a hand. So if a music teacher isn't needed, I'm more than willing to help in any other area.'

After a thoughtful pause, he leaned an elbow on his knee and grinned down at her. A sign of progress. 'I can see you've got the best of intentions, miss, and—'

'Madeline,' she corrected him, and smiled.

The redness in his cheeks seemed to spread. 'It's an admirable gesture you're making, *Madeline*. And I'm sure your friends there would be awfully touched. But I have to tell you, Manzanar isn't the type of place for a sweet, pretty lady like yourself.'

Yet it *was* a place for a sweet, pretty child like Emma?

This wasn't going the way Maddie had hoped. A dead end lay ahead. She would have to switch tactics, no matter how risky.

'Pardon my saying so, Dale' – she spoke with a cordial naivety – 'but if the conditions are acceptable for residents of Japanese descent, surely they're just fine for me. Unless, of course, you're implying that the living standards, per your organization, aren't up to par.'

His teeth clenched around his pipe and his eyes hardened.

The point was made.

'You fill out an application at the reception desk,' he told her, 'and we'll get back to you once an appropriate spot opens up.'

'When?'

In the midst of rising, he huffed a sigh. She knew she was pushing it, but what choice did she have?

'In two weeks. Maybe three. Now, if you'll excuse me.' Grabbing documents from his desk, he returned to the fan. He flipped through the pages, a bald suggestion she leave.

But she didn't. She couldn't. Something told her that if she left this chair, this office today, without her request fulfilled, she'd never see Lane again.

Images of their last exchange shuffled through her mind. She saw the rows of cribs and ironing boards, the Japanese girl being ripped from her adoptive family. What possible threat could the youngster have posed to national security? One-sixteenth of Japanese blood was all it took for exclusion. One-sixteenth. A drop in a filled bucket.

And therein lay her solution.

'Miss,' Dale addressed her, irritated. 'Unless there's something else . . .'

'Actually,' she said, 'there is. You see, I forgot to mention one important detail.'

'Oh? And what would that be?'

She steeled herself – there would be no going back – and through a tightened jaw, she pushed out the lie. 'I'm pregnant,' she said. 'With a Japanese baby.'

PART IV

I am for the immediate removal of every Japanese on the West Coast to a point deep in the interior. . . . Herd 'em up, pack 'em off and give 'em the inside room in the badlands.

Let 'em be pinched, hurt, hungry and dead up against it. . . .

Personally I hate the Japanese. And that goes for all of them.

—Syndicated columnist Henry McLemore

CHAPTER 35

Aside from missing Maddie, hunger was all Lane could think about. Not even the stench of burlap and camo-net dye, compounded with body odor in the factory, could curb his stomach grumbles. Behind the mask covering his mouth, he licked his lips at the memory of shrimp tempura and pickled vegetables. He tasted fresh abalone salad and seaweed-wrapped rice balls.

Things were clearly getting desperate for him to be daydreaming about Japanese staples rather than good ol' American burgers.

Unfortunately, all that awaited today were more impetus for the 'Manzanar Runs': Canned hash and sauerkraut, boiled potatoes too hard to eat. 'Slop suey' that spoiled from refrigeration failures. Evacuees acting as cooks, with little knowledge of cooking.

It was the same routine for every meal. People in line for the mess halls would stare in through the windows. Their famished eyes spurred those inside to rush. Mess tins and forks had replaced elegant bowls and chopsticks. Kids would eat with their friends, same for the parents. Table manners and family meals were things of the past.

Lane's constant appetite, however, sadly remained.

'Hey, Lane,' said the worker next to him. A Burbank native, he used to be an encyclopedia salesman. 'We missed you at the block meeting again.'

'Yeah,' Lane said simply.

The guy nodded in understanding. Together, beneath the twenty-foot ceiling, they used a pulley to raise another net for weaving. Dyed white, it would camouflage tanks in the snow.

'You going to the picture show tonight?' he asked Lane, adjusting his rolled-up sleeves.

Although Lane was willing to do just about anything to break up the monotony – even watch a fuzzy projection on a white sheet in a sandy firebreak – the last film had ruined any allure. *The Hunchback of Notre Dame*. If he'd wanted to see people scorning a love-starved outcast from society, he could have replayed his own memories. 'I don't think so.'

'You sure?'

Lane was about to confirm his answer when he noticed a rash forming on the guy's arms. He'd seen it before, a reaction to the dyes. 'You'd better go see the doc,' he said, pointing to the swollen skin.

'Ah, great.'

The fellow left the factory without seeking

permission. Army engineers were there to supervise, but still this was 'voluntary' work. Sixteen bucks a month for eight-hour days, six days a week. The scenario teetered on the brink of comical. Here they were, unjustly imprisoned by their own country, contributing to the fight for freedom and democracy.

The thought, if nothing else, suppressed Lane's appetite.

'Moritomo-*san!*' A civilian patrolman peeked in from the doorway. 'You got someone here to see you.'

'Who is it?' he hollered back, muffled through his mask.

The man left.

Lane groaned. It had better not be another person trying to convince him to run for block leader. He'd had his fill of government. From Congressman Egan to FDR, they were nothing but performers on a stage – ventriloquists – giving lip service for audience approval.

Shucking off his gloves, Lane threaded his way through workers and equipment to step outside. A low sun scorched the valley and a wave of dust brushed over his eyes. He blinked hard to clear the grit as a throng of schoolgirls strolled past. In their arms, they toted preparations for the annual festivities. Paper lanterns and dragon kites, bright obi to belt their kimonos. Even barbed wire couldn't hinder Obon, a tribute to the dead, an ancestral prayer for good fortune.

For the Moritomo family, of course, it would be just another August day. Lane's mother had discouraged their involvement in the celebration since he was a kid. He couldn't recall why. Evidently mingling with ghosts violated a superstition.

'Somebody here want to see me?' he said over the commotion, and yanked down his mask. No one spoke up. He squeezed his gloves with impatience. Then a hat-covered woman angled toward him, and the sight snagged his breath.

It was Maddie. Here. In front of him.

A smile spread over her lips. Her hair caught a drift of wind, lifting it from the collar of her traveling suit. He knew this outfit, the burgundy number she wore on the train to Seattle. He'd never seen her so beautiful.

Could his mind be playing tricks on him? The heat and desert could do that to a person. So could three months of loneliness.

Tentatively he moved toward her, afraid she was a mirage. 'Maddie?'

Her smile widened, losing none of its sensuality.

He risked breaking the moment by touching her face. She layered her hand over his. The feel of her creamy skin, like satin to his roughened fingers, eliminated any doubt. She indeed was real.

In a reenactment of a scene straight from his dreams, he brushed strands of hair from her neck. Then slowly, to savor the moment, he leaned in for a kiss.

Clang, clang, clang.

The iron triangle announced lunchtime and entrapped him back in Manzanar. His heart twisted like *mochi,* a glutinous mass formed from stretching and pounding. Maddie was never supposed to see him in this godforsaken place.

'Come with me.' He seized her upper arm. He felt her wince, but marched onward to the rec building.

'Honey, what's the matter?'

He gave no explanation upon entering. In a back corner, he released her, though he didn't speak until stragglers sprinted for the bell. 'What are you doing here? I told you not to come. Why didn't you listen?'

Looking confused, Maddie rubbed her arm, where he'd left a handprint of factory dust on her sleeve. The last thing he ever wanted to do was hurt her.

Again, though, that's what he had done.

'I'm sorry,' he said. 'I didn't mean to grab you like that.'

'It's okay . . . it's just tender from the shot.'

The shot?

For typhoid, he concluded in near disbelief. 'So they're making visitors get shots now too? What is that, some new policy because we're so filthy?'

All evacuees had endured a multitude of vaccinations. Emma, like most kids, had taken days for the effects of fever and vomiting to subside. Yet after all that, they weren't considered clean enough.

Maddie stared, a new reaction in her eyes. 'How long has the camp allowed visitors? When you wrote to me, you said . . .'

He knew very well what he had said. White lies flowed easier through a pen.

He crossed over to the window. Work gloves in his grip, he rested a hand on the sill. His reflection in the glass – a dusty, sweaty, blue-collared laborer – confirmed his cause for reservation. This wasn't the man she had married.

'Lane, please. Tell me what's going on.'

He averted his gaze to an American flag flapping in the distance. Alkali stained its white stripes, sunlight bleached the red. How many gusts would it take before the stars simply blew away?

Maddie's shoes clacked on the wooden floor. He didn't know which direction he wished they were moving.

'Sweetheart, listen to me,' she said, close behind him. 'Just like your father, you haven't done anything wrong. You've got nothing to be ashamed of.'

From the words, or her hand on his shoulder, something cracked. An internal shell that had formed without his awareness.

Hesitant, he twisted to face her.

'Don't shut me out,' she told him. It wasn't a plea, but a command. Her eyes, though glowing with warmth, had acquired a new-found strength, powerful enough to override his fear.

After months of separation, pride had no business tainting their reunion.

Lane reached out, as he should have the second he spotted her, and reclaimed her in his arms. The ache in his gut faded away, dissolved by a memory of hope. A reminder of the reward that waited at the end.

He rested his cheek on Maddie's, and whispered in her ear, 'How much time have we got, before visiting hours are over?'

Although he dreaded the answer, there was one thing he knew for certain. The less time she spent here, the better. For her own sake.

'Well,' she said, 'the truth of it is . . .' She drew her head back and her mouth curved upward. 'I'm not exactly visiting.'

CHAPTER 36

Beverly Hills. That's what they called the segregated living area for Manzanar's managing staff, all of the buildings fittingly painted white. Facilities were upgraded, barracks were pristine. Japanese gardeners manicured the grounds.

Maddie wondered how else their conditions differed as she trekked back from the laundry troughs. Trying not to dwell, she focused on the afternoon air rippling above the heated sand. She kept her eyes there while passing two teenage Japanese boys. She had nothing against them in particular. She avoided contact with anyone she didn't know at camp – which, even after several weeks, included everyone but Lane's family.

What good would come of reading in strangers' faces how much she didn't belong? She received enough of that from Kumiko.

Left arm tiring, Maddie adjusted the apple crate of laundered clothing on her hip. She'd folded and ironed each article exactly as her mother had taught her. The woman used to whistle show tunes while pressing her husband's shirts. Maddie would stifle giggles, watching her father sneak in to hug his wife's slender waist.

Would a day ever pass when missing them didn't hurt?

Just then, the wind whipped back a corner of the towel draping the crate. Dust assaulted the exposed garments. Her right hand raised the flattened Oxydol box, a four-foot shield. The carton would be her best peace offering yet, if it didn't soar away before reaching the barrack.

At the intersection, elderly men played Go on a handmade table. Their black and white stones battled in strategy on their gridded game board. A young girl nearby squealed over a hopscotch victory.

Distracted, Maddie stumbled on the bumpy road, but prevented a disastrous fall. In her relief, she glanced up. A mistake. An armed guard in a high wooden tower peered at her from the observation platform. He blew cigarette smoke out the corner of his mouth. Had they been alerted to keep an eye on her, to decide if she were a traitor? Did they suspect she wasn't pregnant?

She imagined an array of consequences. Jail time, a monetary fine, a media frenzy.

Hurrying off, she used the Oxydol box to conceal her waistline. She'd already untucked her blouse as a precaution. If, as she feared, the war crossed the threshold of 1943, a pillow wedged into her skirt could buy a little more time. While her actually conceiving would be ideal, lack of privacy greatly reduced that possibility.

Beside the entry of her barrack, a man paused while trimming his garden. He looked to be in his fifties, wore a Japanese wraparound shirt and straw sandals. According to Lane, he'd started his own flower nursery after serving in the Great War, even earned a Purple Heart while fighting for America.

She opened her mouth to say hello, just as she spotted his left hand. The pinkie and half of his fourth finger were missing. Irrational guilt overcame her. He sent her an amiable look and bowed. Then he returned to his plot, a tidy design of plants and rocks that would help reduce the dust.

She awkwardly tipped her head in kind, though he didn't see her, and she continued inside. There, a pleasant surprise awaited. Lane stood by his cot, fastening the buttons on his jean pants. A sheen of perspiration graced his bare torso. The V of his shoulders had gained definition from long hours at the factory.

When he turned to face her, she felt her skin flush from being caught gawking. Intimacy felt less natural in daylight.

'What are you doing home so early?' she asked, and busied herself with closing the door. She used her foot for lack of a free hand.

'Some meathead spilled dye on me, so I had to change my clothes. Here, I'll help you.'

Maddie let him take both the crate and the cardboard.

'What's this for?' He held up the collapsed Oxydol box before propping it next to the laundry stack.

'It's a little something for your mom.'

His forehead scrunched a question.

'I thought she could use it in the restroom as a divider.' Portable makeshift walls were in high demand for the latrines, all un-partitioned like the showers. Hopefully, the gift would earn Maddie a few points.

Lane bent over and grabbed a clean shirt from the crate. With Kumiko at a painting class and Emma running around with friends, finally Maddie was alone with him. She couldn't recall when that had occurred last, and hated that even this would be short lived.

A yearning propelled her hand to touch his back. 'Can't you stay a little longer?' Her request, without planning, came out breathy and swung him around. A sudden spark in his gaze said he misinterpreted her intentions. She went to clarify, but it dawned on her how much she meant exactly what he'd heard.

As he leaned in, she closed her eyes to welcome his kiss. His mouth joined hers in a motion that fueled desire. Then his lips broke away and his tongue traced the side of her neck. She explored the landscape of his chest and stomach with her fingers. His muscles hardened beneath her touch. He laid her down on his mattress and heat shot through her body.

Only an oil stove separated their cots, yet since her arrival at Manzanar something about him felt unreachable. His initial reaction to her moving here hadn't been the elation she'd expected; he'd mostly voiced concerns over her schooling, her safety.

But any reservations seemed to now burn away in the fire rekindled between them.

Lane's hand traveled under her skirt and up and down her thigh, taking time they normally weren't afforded. For the sake of hot water and crowd avoidance, three A.M. had become Kumiko's regular bathing hour, her absence providing their sole opportunities for romance. Well, as romantic as a couple could get in the span of twelve to fifteen minutes, and with Emma sleeping on the other side of an Army blanket tacked to a beam. No wonder their lovemaking had felt groggy and shameful and rushed. The exact opposite of this moment.

She ran her fingers through his hair. The scent of burning orange peels, meant to drive away mosquitoes, drifted from a neighboring apartment. Wind rattled soup-can lids nailed over knotholes. She grew heady from the certainty of his wanting, his abandon.

Perhaps he had been cautious of getting too comfortable. The uncovering of her charade, just like before, could threaten their reunion.

With her mind rotating on the axis of this revelation, it took her a minute to comprehend that Lane had stopped moving. His breaths fell heavily on her neck. Voices of a married couple resounded off the peaked roof. Their volume was increasing in a standard argument. Once more, the man was accusing her of making eyes at another fellow.

Lane slid away and rose to his feet, the magic dispelled. They weren't alone, after all, and this was no place for abandon. Maddie sat up while tugging her blouse into place. Emma could have walked in at any time. How careless to forget to lock the door.

'I gotta get back to work,' Lane said, pulling on a clean shirt.

She agreed through her discomfort. 'I'll . . . see you at supper, then?'

He answered with a smile, the kind reserved for putting a person at ease, though it only reinstated a maddening sense of distance. He flew out the door without another word.

Pushing down her frustrations, Maddie sought an activity. Any activity. She could always reread her latest letters – reports from Jo on Maddie's house, and Bea about the shop. But those just made her miss her old life more than she already did, and writing them back would mean crafting another glossed-over update. Responding to her brother's post, a demand she return home, wasn't any more appealing. Nor was playing her violin. Musical memories of her father would scarcely lighten her mood.

Her attention shifted to the window. Fingers of a breeze ruffled the polka-dotted apricot curtains. They offered a touch of home, with the practical benefit of blocking nighttime searchlights. She had purchased the material through a Sears, Roebuck catalog, the sewing supplies from the camp's co-op general store. With nervous zeal, she'd presented the accessories to Kumiko, who barely gave them a glance.

To win her approval, Maddie would need to do something drastic. Something Kumiko couldn't ignore.

She rose up on her elbows, her gaze wandering and calculating. The mother and daughter who'd been assigned to their quarters had relocated to Poston, an internment camp in Arizona, to be with their family. The vacancies would allow more spaciousness, given a little scooting of the furniture. That's what Maddie could do – a rearrangement to improve their days together. Maybe they'd all be happier if they weren't literally living on top of one another.

Reenergized, she stood up.

Time to redecorate.

Forty-five minutes later, the job was done. Their beds sat in a new direction, clearing an area that could pass for a parlor. The square table and pair of chairs Lane had made from spare lumber created an invitation for visitors, should they have any, and the hanging blanket now gave Kumiko privacy.

Best of all, the gap between Lane's and Maddie's cots no longer existed.

After dusting the room – a perpetual need with

the cracked planks – a single task remained. Find a good spot for Kumiko's paintings. The woman had accumulated a hefty stack, her specialty being sparrows. Never in flight, always alone, they perched on branches and rocks and rooftops. Maddie was curious about the bird's significance, but her relationship with Kumiko hadn't ripened enough to ask.

Careful not to crease the pictures, Maddie placed them in the Oxydol box and tucked the casing under Kumiko's bed. A temporary solution. The minute Lane returned from his job, she would ask him to build a storage shelf. They could now accommodate more furnishings.

As she stepped back to admire her work, she heard the door open behind her. Emma bounded in, a twinkle in her gaze.

'Hiya, pretty girl,' Maddie exclaimed, eager to unveil her work.

'Close your eyes,' Emma urged. Not yet noticing the room, she held her hands behind her back. 'Go on, close them.'

'All right. But then I have a surprise for you too.'

Emma nodded, and Maddie followed the order. 'Now, put your hands out.'

Maddie raised her cupped palms, praying it wouldn't be a reptile or insect. Thankfully, the object felt inanimate.

'Okay, open them.'

It was an arrowhead the length of her thumb. The black stone – obsidian, Maddie guessed – glistened as she flipped it over. She rubbed the grooves, saddened by the similarities between the Japanese Americans and Paiute Indians. Their people were once exiled from this very desert. 'Emma, this is amazing. Where did you find it?'

'By the old apple orchard.' She accepted the artifact back and studied it in awe. 'Some of the old guys here are collecting them. Hana said I could get fifty cents for it. *Fifty cents!*'

Maddie smiled. 'You could get a lot of Tootsie Rolls for fifty cents.'

'Or,' Emma said, looking up, 'I could buy some new fabric for a dress.'

'That's true, you could. But . . . are you sure your mother won't mind?'

'She only told me I couldn't use my brother's pay to get new clothes. She didn't say anything about my own money.'

Maddie mulled this over. 'I suppose you're right.'

'Would you make it for me? We could pick out a pattern in a catalog,' she suggested. 'Golly, Maddie, it would be sooo nice to wear something new. Even Hana's mom let her buy a new hat for church. Please, please, please?'

How could anyone say no to that?

'Well, all right. But we can only pick out a style your mother would approve of.'

'Thank you, thank you! You're the best.' Emma beamed with a smile that had been gradually fading. After an exuberant hug, she asked, 'Didn't you say you have a surprise for me too?'

The apartment.

Maddie had nearly forgotten. She angled her body out of the way, flinging a hand out to display her creation. 'Ta-da! A whole new house. What do you think?'

Emma glanced around and shook her head. 'We really should move it back.' Her voice was heavy with concern – perhaps at the prospect of another change in her life.

'Oh, Em, I know it'll take some getting used to. But look how nice it is.' Maddie stepped into the parlor and stretched her arms. 'There's so much space, we could put on a circus act. Sell tickets at the door. And hey, just think of all the fabric we could buy from *that* money.'

'We need to put the beds back,' Emma said with growing urgency. 'We have to, before Mother comes home. It's *kita makura*.'

'I – don't understand.'

'*Kita makura*. Our heads can't be to the north. It's bad luck. They only do that for funerals. She'll be furious. We have to hurry.' Emma was already grabbing the foot of Kumiko's cot.

Though stunned, Maddie assisted her. She gained momentum while comprehending the potential backfire of her gesture. She strove to recall each item's original placement. One chair below the window, the other in the corner with the table. The laundry crate got in the way more than once, and the dust they kicked up now blanketed the formerly clean clothes.

They were over halfway done when Emma froze, her hands on the far end of Lane's bed.

'*Nani o shiteruno?*' Kumiko said in a horrified rasp. She stood in the doorway, clutching a small box of painting supplies.

Before Maddie could say a word, Emma launched into Japanese. She inserted Maddie's name twice during what seemed a diplomatic explanation.

Kumiko didn't respond. She just stared at the room, lips sealed, her chest heaving as though preparing to breathe fire.

'Maddie, come on,' Emma whispered, seeking help to place Lane's bed in its cramped corner. Maddie wanted to smooth the situation over herself, but not knowing the extent of Kumiko's English, she continued with their task.

Only when every furnishing had been returned did Kumiko set aside her supplies. From the entry, she walked straight to the folded Oxydol carton leaned up against a wall. She laid it on the table and studied the partition.

At least Maddie had done one thing right.

Kumiko's fingers closed in on her paintings, their corners peeking from the box. She guided them out and a deep red stained her face.

Oh, no. She thought Maddie planned to discard them, along with the empty carton.

'I can explain,' she said to Kumiko, then addressed Emma. 'Please tell her, I was just trying to protect them.'

Emma started to translate, but Kumiko cut

her off. Her words flew like darts, fast and pointed, and her fingers flicked toward Maddie.

'But, *Okāsan* . . . ,' Emma said repeatedly, not being heard.

Maddie moved forward. 'Mrs Moritomo, this is my fault, not Emma's. I didn't mean to offend you. I was only trying to help.'

Kumiko's palm shot up, a universal sign for *stop*. Her eyes skewered Maddie for a stretch of several seconds before she hissed a final phrase at Emma. The air became colder than a December night as she inspected her paintings for damage.

Emma stood there, lip quivering and tears welling. Maddie started to reach for her, to console her and apologize, when Emma pitched the arrowhead across the room.

'*Okāsan nanka daikirai!*' she shouted at her mother, then ran out the door.

Though Maddie didn't understand the language, she recognized the tone.

It was that of a spirit being broken.

CHAPTER 37

'Put a sock in it, "Ravioli,"' TJ grumbled from his seat in the rec hall. If the barracks were cooler, he'd have stayed in there. In which case, he could have written ten letters by now. 'You sound like a blasted cat in heat.'

Unfazed, Ranieri kept right on singing and hula dancing for an audience of airmen. A ground crewman, with just as little talent, strummed a ukulele. As part of some dare for a couple packs of smokes, Ranieri swayed his grass skirt over rolled-up khakis. He swatted at hands groping his coconut-shell brassiere, padded by his curly-haired chest. Throw in a long black wig and he could almost pass as Hula Hattie, the Hawaiian beauty painted on the nose of their B-17.

A disturbing thought, actually.

Even so, when the numskull broke into a Tahitian shimmy, TJ couldn't hold down a smile. Although grateful they'd been assigned to the same crew, based in tropical paradise – whether by sheer luck or the Italian's doings – TJ did wonder how much more peaceful Kahuku Air Base would be without the guy. Boring maybe, but more peaceful.

TJ tore his attention from the tune, so off-key it would have disintegrated Maddie's eardrums, and returned to the letter on the table. He breathed in plumeria on the salty breeze, cleared his head. Pen in hand, he reviewed the last words he'd written to Jo.

Not a whole lot of goings-on here, just the usual practice bombing runs, dull lectures, air raid drills, and whatnot. Vince (that's Ravioli's real name, by the way) and I are going to hitch a ride down to Honolulu this afternoon to catch a double feature. Supposed to be a new one starring Gene Tierney. Even though you've got the girl beat in every way, at least seeing her will remind me of that morning at the station. Boy oh boy, what it does to me just thinking about that whopper of a kiss. All I can hope is that one day we can pick up from where we left off.

Better close now or I'll need a cold shower from more than the island humidity! Take good care, Jo. Keeping you always in my thoughts.
TJ

He sealed the pages in an envelope marked solely with her name. He never bothered with an address, although he knew the hardware store's by heart. Her posts, after all, wouldn't be leaving his footlocker.

Some might consider it strange, penning notes

he had no intention of mailing. But a sense of freedom came with spilling anything he wanted to on paper, a freedom no way he'd feel if his messages were going to be shared. It was like scribbling in a diary, minus the surety of jabs or questions or curious peeks from the fellas. Nobody thought twice about TJ writing letters home, and addressing them to Jo only upped his comfort.

'Aloha, *haole*,' Ranieri sang out. An unlit cigarette peeked from behind one of his ears, a red hibiscus flower from the other. He dropped an orchid lei around TJ's neck. 'About time we got you laid.'

'You need some serious help, pal.'

Ranieri exaggerated a gasp, covering his mouth like a dame. 'And to think, I saved a letter for you at mail call. But now? You can forget it.'

A letter.

Jo Allister.

Had she taken initiative once more? Finally written the first note?

'So hand it over,' TJ said, a little too strong. He yearned to hear from her as much as he feared it.

Ranieri reached into his grass skirt. When he pulled out an envelope, TJ leaned back in his chair. 'Please tell me that was only in your pocket.'

The guy grinned and tossed over the mail – from Maddie, it was only from Maddie.

A good thing, TJ reminded himself. He was doing Jo a favor, leaving her be.

'Better read it lickety-split,' Ranieri told him. 'Kaleo promised us free drinks at his bar if we get to Waikiki early enough.' Maybe due to his dark, Hawaiian-like features, but Ranieri had befriended just about every native on the island.

'Yeah, well, I wasn't the one putting on a vaudeville act,' TJ pointed out. 'And don't think I'm going anywhere with you till you take off those ridiculous coconuts.'

Ranieri studied the shells. 'What, too small for you?' He massaged them in circles and used the pidgin dialect from the locals. 'Handful mo' bettah, brah. Only lolo buggah want humungous bobbi.'

TJ laughed. What other response could he possibly give?

'Be back in ten.' Ranieri sauntered away, presumably to change clothes.

With time to spare, TJ opened his sister's letter. He anticipated her usual updates woven with nudges about Lane, some more subtle than others. He made it through three sentences before his eyes jumped back to the opening.

Dear TJ,
I know that what I am about to tell you will surely disappoint you, but please understand I must follow my heart. I have given my decision a great deal of thought. Even if you were here, rest assured I would have done this regardless.

Suspense from the disclaimers spurred him to skim. Two-thirds down the page he discovered what she'd done.

'The hell you're not!'

Faces turned in his direction.

He didn't finish. He'd read enough. Grabbing the pages, he stormed off, dead set on getting Maddie home.

Lieutenant Colonel Stone sat at his desk, flipping through paperwork that had nothing to do with TJ's request. He spoke without looking up. 'Afraid I can't help you, Corporal, unless you fill me in.'

'The emergency involves my sister's safety, sir.'

'And what *precisely* would that emergency be?'

In the center of the office, TJ gripped his wrist behind his back, wanting direly to strangle something. Or someone. 'Sir, it's a – personal matter.'

The squadron commander chuckled as if entertained by an inside joke. Gray smoke wended upward from a cigarette on the man's overflowing ashtray. Finally he raised his eyes. 'See, now, that's the beauty of belonging to the Army. We're one big happy family, which means there *are* no personal matters. At least not until you add a few more stripes to your sleeve.' His lips flattened below his thick mustache.

The joke was over.

'Way I see it,' he went on, 'you either tell me what's got your drawers in a bunch, or you can pack up your furlough request and get your butt out of my office. I got work to do.'

With TJ's usual chains of command out on training flights for the day, he needed the man's approval to get clearance off the island. Minus that and he'd be facing a court-martial. He'd be no good to his sister from a jail cell.

TJ tried not to cringe as he shoved out the explanation. 'Our parents are deceased.' In essence, the truth. 'And my sister has followed her husband, a Japanese American, to live in a relocation center on the mainland. That's why I just need long enough to travel there and move her back home. I'm sure I don't have to tell you that her life's in danger.' That was it. All the essentials – except for one: 'Sir.'

Gradually, Stone reclined in his chair. 'Well, that's not one I hear every day.' He peaked a thick brow. 'I don't suppose this is some cockamamie excuse for wanting to buzz back and see your sweetheart?'

'I wish it were.'

The officer exhaled through his nose, contemplating. 'I've got a sister myself. She's working as a riveter in some aircraft factory. Didn't listen to a dang thing I said about those dangerous jobs being for others. So, Corporal, I do understand where you're comin' from.'

'Thank you, sir.' TJ managed a level tone, concealing his relief. He could already see himself on a train, riding back to L.A. with Maddie. Maybe now, after actually living in the camp, she wouldn't be hard to persuade.

Then Stone said, 'That's why I'm real sorry I can't help you.'

A sucker punch to the gut.

'We've got special missions coming up, and I won't be able to spare a single one of ya. Definitely not for that long. And no chaplain I know is going to override this one, if that's what you're thinking.'

'But, sir—'

'You want her home? You help us win this war and that's exactly where she'll end up. In the meantime, you just write her the best letter you can, and above all, keep her in your prayers.' The commander paused before slapping on a 'Dismissed,' then huddled over his documents.

TJ remained in place, anchored by defeat. Finally he gathered the strength to move toward the exit.

'And just so you know,' Stone added, 'I think it's a shame.'

TJ's grip stopped on the door handle. He didn't need his embarrassment stoked over the matter. Solely for protocol, he glanced back.

'My parents' best friends are living in one of them camps,' Stone said. 'The Ishinoyas. Decent, hardworking people. Don't deserve what they're gettin'.' He shook his head. 'Like I said, a real ugly shame.'

CHAPTER 38

In the doorway of his apartment, Lane scowled at the awaiting welcome. A Nisei man stood in a brown and tan uniform, nightstick in his belt, white *POLICE* band around his arm. As the guy attempted to communicate with Lane's mother – his Japanese sounded broken – Emma sat on her cot. She sent her Mary Janes a look of boredom, scuffing the leather toes on an inch-wide crack in the floor.

Nothing pointed to an emergency. No FBI raid or arrest. Just another wrist-slapping for his sister.

Still, Lane didn't need this today. A colicky infant in their barrack had been robbing him of what little sleep he could finagle. And more than tired, he was hungry after a long day of monotonous work.

'What's she done this time?' he muttered.

The civilian officer looked over. His face, shaped like an eggplant, showed relief at Lane's arrival.

'Has she been skipping more classes?'

'Afraid that's only part of our problem.'

Lane shot a glance at his sister, whose shoulders suddenly drooped. Truth be told, he couldn't blame her for avoiding school here. Lessons were held in a rec building, as short on teachers as they were supplies. But her education had been a major lure to the camp, which meant she sure as heck better show up.

'As I was trying to tell your mother here,' the officer said, gesturing toward the table where she now sat, 'it's about your sister and some kids from San Pedro – a pretty rowdy group, I might add. Seems they've all been mess-hall hopping again. Three or four times a meal, according to my reports.'

Lane asked Emma, 'Is this true?'

She hesitated, shrugged.

'Emma, for crying out loud. We've talked about this. You're not supposed to eat anywhere but in our block.'

'And I would,' she said, 'if ours didn't taste like doggie doo.' A roll of her eyes made clear just how much her demeanor had soured, and not just tonight. 'You know our cook used to be a barber, don't you? He can't even make rice the right way.'

Not a bit of her statement rang false, but pressure from his mother's gaze, along with the policeman's, called for Lane's sternness. 'You eat the food you're given or you won't eat at all. I don't care if the meals taste like dirt. You're lucky to have them. Understand?'

'Fine. Then I'll starve.'

The challenge at first shook him, then pricked him with anger. The loss of control in all parts of his life was enough to drive his fist through their tarpaper wall.

'Is everything all right?' Maddie's voice entered.

He didn't turn toward her. This was a private affair, a moment of familial embarrassment. He'd never invited her to see any of this.

'There's one more thing,' the officer said. 'We don't have a name, but we believe a kid in your sister's gang is responsible for an incident yesterday. It involved the ladies' showers in block ten. A couple lizards were tossed into the stall. Caused quite a ruckus.'

The visual of screaming women jumping around in the showers, all to avoid a pair of harmless reptiles, would have struck Lane as comical a few months back. But humor had since escaped him.

'It won't happen again.' The graveness of his pledge appeased the officer, who traded small bows with Lane's mother.

'Have a good evening, ma'am,' the guy said to Maddie, and closed the door behind him.

The perfect ending to a perfect day.

Lane stepped toward Emma. 'You're grounded. From now on, Maddie will walk you to and from school. You'll eat with no one but your family. Other than the showers and bathroom, you don't leave this barrack.'

Emma stood up, devastated. 'But I didn't have anything to do with the lizards. Cross my heart, I really didn't.'

From the look on her face and plea in her tone,

he believed her. Yet that didn't matter. With their father under suspicion, it wouldn't take much to further tarnish the family's standing. A man's name, as their mother always said, was no less precious than skin to a tiger. To reestablish their worth, the Moritomos needed to act better than everyone else.

'It was that dummy with the spiky hair,' Emma went on explaining. 'When he brought up the idea, I told him not to.'

'I don't want to hear it,' Lane ground out.

'But at least let me tell you—'

'*Urusai!*' He'd heard enough.

Hurt sprang into her round face. He'd always listened when she asked, never treated her like a baby.

All that was before.

Gently, Maddie touched his forearm. 'Honey, please. She deserves a chance to tell her side.'

Deserve? The word had lost any value. No one in this family deserved to be here, yet here they were.

'Emma doesn't *deserve* anything. She's a kid. She needs to do what she's told.'

'Lane,' she said, 'you're her brother.' *Not her father*, he could hear her thinking.

He felt his chest stretch in defiance. 'Well, in case you haven't noticed, our father isn't exactly around.'

As he spoke, doubts planted deep inside shot up like weeds. Doubts he didn't even know were there:

Why *wasn't* the man here? Other detainees had been released and rejoined their families at Manzanar. All that their own family received were periodic letters from their father, idle talk censored with black markers or scissors. What words had been cut out? If Nobu Moritomo was innocent, wouldn't the Justice Department have let him go by now?

Emma dropped hard onto her cot. She snatched her Sarah Mae doll into her arms. 'You're acting so *bōtchie*,' she grumbled at Lane.

Japanesey. That's what she'd called him, as if the rest of them were actually something else. The only real exception was Maddie, whose very presence made him feel more Japanese than ever.

'I wish Papa were here,' Emma said to her doll, each word a puncture to Lane's soul. A flood of emotion burst through him.

'Oh, yeah?' he said. 'Well, Papa's never coming back, so you'd better get used to me being in charge.'

'*Takeshi!*' His mother jumped to her feet. It was her first sign of passion about anything in months.

Emma glared at him, sharp with fear. 'That's a lie. Take it back.'

He opened his mouth to soften the impact, but couldn't. His declaration, he realized, could very well be the truth.

At his silence, a whimper leaked from Emma's throat, a heart-wrenching sound. Mother started to reach for her, then pulled back. She gave way

293

for Maddie to sit on the bed and hug the girl to her side.

That used to be Lane's role. The comforter. Now he was the bad guy. What other significance did he have?

TJ, Dewey . . . heck, half the guys from Lane's old neighborhood were serving in the military. Fighting back, making a difference. And here he was, coloring nets for a living. At sixteen bucks a month, he was a mindless volunteer, a husband pretending to provide. He couldn't even be intimate with his wife as a real man should.

The thoughts grew smothering. The walls were closing in.

Needing to breathe, he left the room.

Above the mountain range, grayness mottled the October sky. The makings of a daily thunderstorm. Five lines of barbed wire ran parallel to Lane's path, each connecting wooden posts in the ground. Nearly two feet spanned each opening. Guided by an urge, he angled his walk, edged a bit closer to the perimeter that screamed with a sign.

EVACUEES
STAY 10 FT. AWAY FROM FENCE

The closest guard tower sat a good hundred yards away. No older than eighteen, the GI held his rifle in the tedious, clumsy manner of a city kid manning a hoe. Would he actually have the gumption to shoot if a prisoner made a run for it?

'Where are you going?' Maddie demanded, catching up to him. Displeasure burned in her eyes.

'Maddie, please stay out of this.'

'You need to talk to your sister. To tell her you didn't mean what you said.'

'This is between me and my family, all right?'

She narrowed her eyes. 'And I'm not part of your family?'

'That isn't what I—' Frustration brewed inside, tightening his jaw. 'You just don't understand our culture.'

They stared through a tense pause. Then she took a step back, looking equally stern and hurt. 'You're right. I don't understand all of it. But more than that, I don't understand *you.*'

She tramped away, headed for their barrack. A pathetic excuse of a home. If he'd been more truthful in his letters to her, described the real conditions at camp, would she still have been willing to come? To make the sacrifices she had?

Those with Japanese heritage didn't have a choice of being incarcerated. Maddie did.

Your wife sure must love you, guys at the factory had told him. Although meant as a compliment, a sign of acceptance, the remark further tipped the scales of his unbalanced marriage. What did he possibly have left to offer her?

A cattle call for supper rang through the desert,

launching another meal session for a crowd of ten thousand. Lane wandered away from the growing mass, his appetite lost to a dose of irony: In the confines of but one square mile, he was losing everyone he loved, as well as himself.